HOSTAGE

HOSTAGE

Ted Allbeury

This title first published in Great Britain 2003 by
SEVERN HOUSE PUBLISHERS LTD of
9–15 High Street, Sutton, Surrey SM1 1DF.
Originally published in 1984 in Great Britain
under the title *No Place to Hide*.
This title first published in the USA 2004 by
SEVERN HOUSE PUBLISHERS INC of
595 Madison Avenue, New York, N.Y. 10022.

British Library Cataloguing in Publication Data

Allbeury, Ted, 1917-
    Hostage
    1.   Intelligence officers - Great Britain - Fiction
    2.   Kidnapping - Fiction
    3.   Suspense fiction
    I.   Title
    823.9'14 [F]

ISBN 0-7278-6037-2

Printed and bound in Great Britain by
MPG Books Ltd., Bodmin, Cornwall.

With love to Thys Ockersen – citizen of Amsterdam
– the most civilised city in Europe.

Law is a regulation in accord with reason, issued by a lawful superior for the common good.

Thomas Aquinas, *Summa Theologicae*

Chapter 1

THE MAN was tall, just over six feet, and his face, chest and shoulders were a deep brown. The tan that comes from wind as well as sun. He was in his early forties, his black hair already beginning to streak with grey, but his body was firm and well muscled. He was wearing a pair of khaki shorts, and shoes without socks. Down the slope of the hill from the small wooden house he could see three cars parked by the stall where they sold the eggs and produce from the small-holding.

They had lived there for nearly two years, earning a bare living from the tourists heading for South Hero from mainland Burlington. They came in their hundreds to Lake Champlain and many of them stopped at the stall to buy stores for their week's holiday. In the spring and fall the trees and foliage of Vermont brought visitors from all over the States. The leaves were already beginning to turn gold and red but there would be another two months before they packed up the stall for the winter.

The locals on the other small scattered farmsteads had been good to them right from the start, helping him to repair the ramshackle clapboard house, letting him join the local farm cooperative so that he could buy poultry food, fertiliser and seed at discount, digging them out from the snow that first terrible winter.

There was another hour's light and he turned to go back to the barn and the tractor. There was something wrong with the linkage on the PTO and it would save him 40 dollars if he could put it right himself. With neither mechanical nor farming skills he had had to learn from instruction manuals and textbooks, and despite the practical difficulties that came from ignorance he had found peace and calm from the new life. He often wondered whether the peace came from the farm or from the girl. She would go on selling until it was too dark to see. He smiled to himself as he worked. For a girl who loathed capitalism, cities, governments and the establishment she neverthless enjoyed selling their produce. The fact that she was young and pretty helped, but she swore that it was the reputation of their fresh eggs and luscious organically-grown fruit that made the tourists come back for more.

He went round the poultry arks before the light went, closing them for the night and taking half a dozen eggs for their own meal from the nesting boxes.

He was soaping his body under the shower when he heard her come into the house and a few minutes later he walked into the living room, a towel round his waist.

She was twenty-three, twenty-four in two months' time, and she was strikingly pretty. Even prettier than when he had first met her when she was barely twenty. She turned to look at him.

'I took 352 dollars, honey. Everything's gone. I've got two people coming back tomorrow for more eggs.'

'Well done, kid. I'll do an early egg-collection tomorrow. They're doing well, those hybrids. Averaging 200 eggs a bird and still two months to go. And all top size with strong white shells.'

She laughed softly as she looked up at his face. 'I never thought you'd stick it. I knew you'd try – but I thought you'd miss so much.'

'Like what?'

She shrugged. 'Theatres . . .'

'I never went to the theatre. It bores me stiff. I prefer the movies.'

She laughed. 'We've been to the movies three times in fourteen, no, fifteen months. That's all. What about England? Don't you miss England?'

'I never think about it, let alone miss it. That's all over.'

'What about your daughters?'

She regretted saying it the moment it was said. Those muscles stiffening at the sides of his mouth and the pulse

8

beating by his left eye. But if she didn't ask he could think she wasn't aware or didn't care.

'They're better off without me.' He paused, shaking his head like a dog coming out of water, as if to shake away the thoughts in his mind. 'How about I do us an omelette. I've brought in some eggs.'

'OK. Suits me fine.'

He stood with his hands on his hips looking at her face.

'How about you, honey. Are you bored?'

'Me? You're crazy. I'm the confirmed dropout, it's you who's the city slicker.'

He shrugged. 'It's fine longing for the simple life when you're in New York or London. Or Amsterdam for that matter. But it ain't necessarily the same when you've actually got it.'

'It's great, Johnny. I love it, every minute of it.'

'What do you love?'

'Jesus. Everything. No crowds, no muggers, no guys trying to push me drugs because they want to screw me. No self-important creeps in offices playing God so I can earn a hundred bucks a week.' She paused and then said, softly, 'I always meant it, Johnny. This is where I belong.' She smiled. 'And here I've got you. And I love you, mister. You're the only really honest person I've met. And you're the only man who's ever actually listened to what I say.'

She slid her warm arms around his neck and kissed him avidly, her young body pressed to his.

It seemed a long time and a long way from those sleazy rooms in Amsterdam. The blue pills to fight off the depression, the temptation to call it a day in the dark, cold waters of the Amstel river.

Chapter 2

HE HAD recognised the face as soon as he saw him but he couldn't place him for several minutes. At first he assumed it was one of their distant neighbours, and then the penny dropped. His name was Logan or Cogan. Something like that. And the last time he had seen him Logan had been one of the agents on a refresher course he was instructing at Moulton House. He'd been talking to them about covert room searches without a full back-up team. Logan had asked him some questions about under-carpet pressure pads. It all seemed a long time ago but it must be only a couple of years. Maybe three.

There had been a hold up on the road from the mainland across the lake to the island. A big Dodge truck had broken down and two patrolmen were trying to sort out the shambles as impatient weekend trippers vented their frustration by revving engines and blaring horns. He had walked back down the line of cars to talk to old man Swenson, and Logan had been at the wheel of an elderly Chev saloon.

As he walked back to his own car he looked across the lake to where the orchards of South Hero were bathed in the evening sun. After nearly two years of peace he had tended to assume that either they didn't know where he was, or that they had decided to leave him alone. But they hadn't sent Logan all the way from London to Vermont just to sample the fresh apple cider and apple and pumpkin pie that South Hero was famous for. He sighed as he got back in the car.

When the long tail-back of vehicles eventually moved on he didn't turn off to the cabin road but went on past South Hero, through Keeler Bay and on up to Grand Isle. The dark blue Chevy followed about a quarter of a mile behind.

Rennie drove fast into the next corner and turned sharp left to the Lovell's barn, cut the engine and looked in the driving mirror. The SIS man drove past, staring ahead, but Rennie waited until it was dark before he turned back down the road to South Hero and the farmstead.

There were 62 typed pages in the cardboard box-file. He had written it all out by hand and then typed it himself on the second-hand Olivetti Lettera. The writing had taken him four days and three nights. It was checking the dates that took the time. And the typing had taken a week.

On the outskirts of Winooski he slowed down at the long row of single-storey shops and offices, and then he saw what he was looking for. The hand-painted sign said, 'DIY Xeroxing 10¢ a sheet'. He pulled in and stopped the car. The old man who owned the general store offered to let his daughter do the copying but Rennie thanked him and did it himself. It took him until well past lunch-time before the seven sets of copies were done. He bought stout brown envelopes and put a set in each and sealed them from a roll of Scotch tape, crossing the length and breadth of each envelope three times.

He drove to the next public phone. What he wanted was a young attorney who'd be eager for the business and wouldn't want to ask a lot of questions. He called the operator and gave the story of trying to trace this newly qualified lawyer from Yale or Harvard, he couldn't remember which. The operator didn't know the background details of any lawyers but from the new subscribers' list she gave him the phone numbers and addresses of the two newest attorneys in Winooski.

He chose the nearest. A Howard Bernstein, whose place was over a dry-cleaning store. An elderly secretary announced his arrival and he was shown in straightaway to the inner office.

Bernstein looked about thirty, soberly dressed in a dark grey suit and a dark red tie, but his face was the face of a shrewd and eager operator. The rows of law-books behind him looked brand-new as he waved Rennie to the comfort-

able leather chair in front of his desk.

'What can I do for you Mr . . . ?'

'Novaks. Paul Novaks. I just want to put some documents into safe-keeping.'

Bernstein smiled. 'Wouldn't a safe-box at one of the banks be cheaper, Mr Novaks?'

'Well there's a possibility that there could be a question of forwarding the documents to certain people if . . . if it became necessary.'

'Are those the documents? The ones you've got there?'

'Yes. They're already addressed to various organisations. You'd just have to post them if you were asked to.'

'Sounds simple enough. How long are you likely to want them kept here?'

'Indefinitely.'

'And you would pay periodically, I take it?'

'No. I'd like to make a once-and-for-all payment. I'd got in mind two thousand dollars.'

Bernstein tried not to look surprised. 'Why did you come to me, Mr Novaks?'

'Somebody recommended you.'

Bernstein's face showed some disbelief. 'Who was that?'

'I don't remember.'

'I see. Well I don't see any problem. I'll give you a receipt for the documents and a receipt for the money.'

Bernstein held out his hand and Rennie put all but two of the packets on his desk. Bernstein glanced at the address of the top one. It just said, 'The Editor, The Washington Post, 1150, 15th St NW, Washington DC.' Bernstein glanced briefly back at Rennie, then pulled over his pad and picked up a pen.

Rennie said, 'I don't need a receipt for the documents nor for the fee. I'll be paying cash.'

Bernstein shrugged and watched as Rennie counted out twenty used hundred-dollar bills. He made no attempt to count them himself but said, 'You'd be calling for the documents personally when you want them?'

'No. It probably wouldn't be me. It would be a girl who'd come for them. Or maybe she'd just phone you.'

'I see. Could I have the lady's name?'

13

'She'd just give you a message. Only she would know the message so there'd be no doubt she was the right person.'

Bernstein picked up his pen. 'I'd better take the message down and put it with the documents.'

'No. I don't want that. It's just a simple message. I'd like you to remember it.'

'What is it?'

'She'll say she wants the documents sent off, and when you ask her to identify herself she'll say, "Should old acquaintance be forgot and never brought to mind".'

Bernstein looked at Rennie's face. 'What if something happens to me?' he said quietly. 'I could get knocked over by a car.'

'I'll take the risk, Mr Bernstein.'

Bernstein was aware of the fact that his client had not expressed any hope that he might not be hit by a car and as he looked at his visitor's face he realised that what had at first sight seemed soft, brown, spaniel's eyes were, in fact, hard and strangely compelling. For a moment he hesitated and then he said, 'D'you live around these parts, Mr Novaks?'

'I'm just visiting. Passing through.' And Rennie stood up, proffering his hand to the lawyer. Bernstein's hand was dry and his grip strong and Rennie felt confident that the young man would carry out conscientiously the instructions he had given him.

Rennie drove down to Burlington and booked a seat on the Delta evening flight to Washington.

Rennie stood looking out at the lights and bustle of the city from the window of the hotel bedroom. He hated being away from the peace of the small farm. And he hated being away from her. But he knew it had to be done. The loneliness was the price of the insurance policy. But being alone in a hotel bedroom reminded him of what it used to be like. In Berlin and Paris, Hamburg and Bangkok, Beirut and Tel Aviv, Brazil and Addis Ababa. And Amsterdam of course. A week or two planning, moving from one hotel to another, then a few hours aimlessly hanging about until it was time to do whatever had to be done. Checking watches, a last look at a street map and instinctively reaching to touch the pistol in the holster under his left arm. The pistol that was now wrapped in oily rags and a plastic bag under the straw and floorboards of one of the poultry arks. It had 'Smith and Wesson' engraved on its barrel. Model 39-2. But it was a long way from its original specification . Three hundred pounds' worth of mods that had made it a killer's weapon and the Guttersnipe sight that made its accuracy almost incredible for a hand-gun.

There were crumpled pages of notepaper in the waste-paper basket by the small table and he turned from the window and walked back to the chair and sat down as he switched on the bedside lamp. The brief note to the ambassador asking him to forward the packet in the diplomatic bag was already done and sealed in its envelope. It was the letter to Paynter that was the problem. Rennie wasn't a natural letter-writer and he was uncertain about what he should say. He was torn between anger and the need to make it work. He tried to imagine Paynter's reaction as he sat in his office and read the letter and then his detailed documentation of every 'dirty-tricks' operation that he had carried out personally for SIS. It was almost another hour before he started writing the note for the last time.

To: G.S. Paynter. Dep. Dir. Special Services.
From: J.H. Rennie.

Enclosed is a copy of the material that will be sent to the media by third parties if there should be any harassment of any kind of myself or the girl. J.H.R.

He read it through a dozen times, tempted to add to the threat or express his anger at what they had done to his life. But he had been in the business a long time and he knew it was enough.

Chapter 3

HE STOOD listening in the silence of the woods. And as he waited, the woods came slowly back to life. Two wood-pigeons cooing softly, the flutter of wings in the tops of the trees, and far away in the distance the faint sound of a dog barking. Then he could hear it, the cracking of dry twigs and branches as Hartmann headed towards him, running away from Williams who was probably more scared than Hartmann himself. But not so scared he wouldn't carry out his orders. Williams had taken a double-first at St Anthony's. Russian and German. But he had been hope-less at even the mildest rough stuff so they'd put him behind a desk to evaluate documents in peace and quiet.

But Attwood in Hamburg had gone down with his annual dose of amoebic dysentery and Williams had been sent out to help him with Hartmann. He had been quite good on the planning and analysis but when, inevitably, it had come to putting on the pressure Williams couldn't take it.

Rennie could hear Hartmann's heavy breathing as the German clambered over fallen tree trunks, weeping in desperation as he cursed the thorns that snatched at his clothes. He could see him now, looking at the ground, stumbling as he ran, no thought of looking to see if there was anyone else but Williams. He let him almost pass the tree and then reached out, confidently and efficiently, and one strong arm locked round Hartmann's fat neck from behind. Hartmann tried to scream but no sound came from his lips as the hard wrist jerked back against his throat. There was always a temptation to say something before you did it. Explain why it was happening. That they hadn't got away with it. But it wasn't professional. When it had gone that far there was no point in underlining whatever mistake they had made. No point in sermonising.

As Hartmann's large plump body wriggled in the grip of Rennie's right arm, Rennie's left arm came up, the hand gently cupping the German's chin to measure the distance. Then the thumb slid up, along the angle of the jaw to the nerve behind the ear, the folds of flabby flesh parting reluctantly until he could feel the apex of the bone. His shoulders shook with the effort as his thumb pressed against the nerve and he staggered back a step under the weight of Hartmann's unconscious body. Then Hartmann's body seemed to ripple, every muscle moving involuntarily, and there was the stench as his bowels voided noisily.

As he lowered Hartmann's body to the wet leaves Williams arrived, panting, the gun in his hand, staring down at Hartmann's corpse before he looked up at Rennie's face.

'Is he dead?'

'Of course he's dead.'

'How did it happen?'

Rennie said softly, 'It didn't *happen*, Roger. I *did* it.'

'What are we going to do with him?'

'We'll leave him here.'

'But he could lie here for days before somebody finds him.'

'So what. He's dead and that's all that matters.'

Williams shook his head slowly. 'I've never understood you, Johnny. None of you people. How the hell do you sleep at nights?'

'Go through his clothes and see if there's anything you want for the office.'

For ten minutes Williams gingerly slid his hand into various pockets and checked the contents. Then he stood up, holding out Hartmann's wallet.

'D'you want this?'

'Why should I?'

'There's nearly three thousand D-marks in it.'

'I don't steal from dead bodies, Roger. Put it back where it came from . . . and if there's nothing you want then we'd better get moving. Back to the car.'

They were sitting in the flat in Grosse Bleicher, the curtains flapping slowly at the open window in the soft summer breeze that came off the Binnen Alster. The noise of the traffic just audible.

Williams looked at Rennie's face and said, 'Don't you ever get sick of it . . . all the violence?'

'It isn't all violence. In fact, there's very little violence.'

'But all the messing about. Finding out how to pressure them. Trying to find out if they screw young boys, or underaged girls, all the perversions. The filth that people get up to.'

Rennie shrugged. 'It isn't always that sort of thing. That's just your nasty mind. Some of them are selling things they shouldn't be selling. Sophisticated missiles to crazy governments. Like Gadaffi, for instance. Forging documents so that a Red Brigade loony can assassinate some country's Foreign Minister just for a few paragraphs in the world's press. Or the IRA shooting fathers in front of their wives and kids. Why do you always have to let your heart bleed for the villains?'

'Is that what they tell you when they're training you?'

'I didn't need telling. It's my country I'm protecting. A damn good country. The best in the world in my opinion. You don't keep your freedom if you won't fight for it. Every minute of every hour there's a dozen bastards planning to bring us down. To hand us over to foreigners of some kind or another.'

'Is it really that black and white? Hartmann for instance.'

'My God, Roger. How can you say that? Franz Ludwig Hartmann was a Nazi. Right from the start. Not when you had to be a Nazi to keep your job, but in 1933. He bought out Jewish businesses for a song. Took their heirlooms in return for documents that were supposed to get them to the USA. Except that most of them ended up in Dachau or Belsen or some other bloody camp.

'When the war ends he's a rich man. He bribes all and sundry to hide his identity. Moves up here to Hamburg. Gets elected to the Town Council, then to Bonn. Is appointed to a sensitive committee that deals with NATO secrets. The Russians trace him, blackmail him, and he

19

passes over every document he can lay hands on that's of any importance. What did you want us to do? Tell him not to be a naughty boy?'

'But it's the Germans' business, surely. And the due process of law.'

'The Germans knew, for Christ's sake. But it would have meant one more scandal for an already shaky party. They've had enough scandals of Soviet agents in Cabinet offices. And he had friends in the right places. He'd spent tens of thousands of dollars seeing that he had friends in the right places.

'Of course they were going to deal with him. It was just a question of timing, they said. That was three months ago.'

'But they'll know we did it.'

'Of course they will. And they'll be delighted that we've got rid of the problem for them. They've got plenty more problems where he came from and they'd be only too glad for us to solve them the same way.'

'Were you recruited straight into SIS?'

'No, I read law, practised for a year, and then I did four years in the army. SAS.'

'It doesn't worry you, the dirty tricks?'

'I'm not employed to worry, my friend. I've got every faith in the people above me who decide these things. Whatever they give me to do, I do. You can't have a discussion group about democracy and fair play every five minutes when you're dealing with bastards like Hartmann.'

'And due process of law? That doesn't count for anything?'

Rennie smiled. 'Some High Court judge once said that the judges were there not to administer justice but to administer the law. Why should we go through all that humbug when we know what they've done and what they deserve?'

'You think that the law is humbug?'

'In these sorts of things, yes. Just expensive barristers running up the bills. A hundred thousand quid of the public's money to try and prove that a well-known terrorist really is a terrorist. It would be laughable if it wasn't so serious.'

'You never have any doubts?'

Rennie shook his head slowly. 'Never. Why should I? The people who give me my assignments are responsible for the security of the country. If they say that's what is needed, I do it. To the very best of my ability.'

'You'd carry out any order they gave you?'

'Of course.'

'Say they're wrong sometime and some innocent guy ends up floating in the canal face down?'

'That's not for me to decide. I can't know everything they know.'

'So even if you knew the guy was innocent you'd knock him off?'

'If those were my orders, yes. They don't go after innocent men. Why the hell should they?'

'Maybe he's innocent but they just don't like him. Or maybe they're mistaken.'

'Too bad.'

'D'you sleep at nights OK?'

'Like a log.'

'They must love you, Johnny.'

'They respect me and I respect them. Loyalty counts for a lot. Chaps like you are always full of doubts. Never sort yourselves out. You should remember what Cromwell told his men.'

'What was that?'

'Know what you fight for, and love what you know.'

'Sounds ghastly. When are you going back to London?'

'Have you got a Canadian passport I can use?'

'United States do?'

'OK. In that case I'll go tomorrow.'

'D'you fancy a night out with a couple of pretty girls?'

'No thanks.'

'You still carrying a torch for Mary?'

'No way.' Rennie shook his head vigorously.

'Let's go eat at the Four Seasons.'

'OK.'

Chapter 4

BORA GLEN village lies between what the locals call The Gowls and Big Torr, the two massive hills whose valley points towards the Forth estuary. The village streets have been cobbled since the 1600s and the architecture of even its humbler homes was decided by the local orange-tinted stone and the Dutch tiles that came over to the Fife harbours on boats from the Low Countries.

The Rennies' house was at the northern end of the village where the road led to the awe-inspiring gorge formed by the rift in the Ochil Hills. It had always been known as the Little Manse although it had never housed a minister when James Rennie moved in with his new bride. The deep and misshapen scar on James Rennie's left cheek was a permanent reminder of the last months of World War I. On his release from hospital the shortage of trained teachers had led to his appointment as headmaster of the village school. He was almost forty when he married the much younger girl who bore him their only child, a son. The school provided both primary and secondary education for nearly two hundred children from the villages that were scattered along the valley and the hills. Not even the rose-pink spectacles of nostalgia had ever persuaded an alumnus to admit to a moment's pleasure in his time at the school. But their successes at the university in Edinburgh and in their future lives had made a reputation for the ex-captain headmaster. Four rugby caps for Scotland, a bishop, a raft of cabinet ministers; city money-men gladly sent cheques when the school appealed for funds; but they never went back.

John Hamish Rennie had been afraid of his father until

he was eight years old. Physically and mentally afraid. The sight of his father's tall, gaunt frame approaching could bring him near to fainting. He was aware that his father despised his spindly weak body and his ineptitude at both learning and games. He spoke only when spoken to but that was not unusual in those parts.

It all changed with the chickens. His father kept a dozen Rhode Island Reds in a shed in the back-garden and on a Friday evening in the summer before his ninth birthday he had been picking flowers for his mother when his father called him over. He was inside the chicken shed.

His father said, without turning to look at him, 'Hold the door open, laddie, and give me some light.'

As he held the door his father stooped and grabbed a hen's legs, its wings flapping as he tucked it under his arm. Two big hands twisted in opposite directions on the chicken's neck and held it until the twitching body was still. His father turned and held out the dead hen. 'Take it to your mother, boy. Tell her I'll pluck it later.' He held the boy's arm and looked at his pale face as he shrank back. 'Ye're no' frightened of a dead hen, are ye, lad?'

'Yes, father.'

The man looked intently at the boy's face and then said quietly. 'Come straight back here when ye've handed over the bird.'

'Yes, father.'

When the boy returned his father had another hen tucked under his arm. He pointed at its neck.

'Take hold of its neck with both hands.'

And as the boy's hands closed round the thin warm neck his father said, 'Go on. Wring its neck. Twist like I did. Hard.'

The bird squawked and shrieked and struggled under the man's arm. Then its neck went limp. As the boy stood there he looked up at his father's face. His father was smiling and he said softly, 'Well done, laddie. Take it to the kitchen then I want to see you in my study. Wash your hands first.'

His father had lit the old oil-lamp in his study and he sat in the big oak upright chair alongside the circular mahogany table. He beckoned the boy over and he stood in front

24

of the man.

'What do you think of ma face, laddie? Here.' And he pointed at the massive scar.

'I'm sorry about it, sir.'

'You know how I got it?'

'In the Great War, sir. A piece of a shell.'

'Ugly isn't it?'

The boy stood silent.

His father said softly, 'I'm proud of that scar, laddie. Look at the wee box on the table.'

The boy reached out for the small leather box and his father said, 'Go on. Open it.'

The boy looked at the mauve stripe on the white ribbon and the metal cross with a crown on each spur. He looked back at his father's face.

'Do you know what it is?'

'It's a medal, sir.'

'It's a Military Cross and that's why I'm proud of my ugly face. The King himself gave it to me. At Buckingham Palace. Your mother was with me. D'you know why I'm showing it to you today?'

'No, sir.'

'Because when I asked you if you were scared of a dead hen you told me the truth. And because you wrung the chicken's neck when I told you to. You *were* scared, weren't you?'

'Yes, sir.'

'But you're not scared to do it again, are you?'

'No, sir.'

'Would you do it again if I told you to right now?'

The boy nodded. 'I would, sir.'

The man pointed at the medal in its case. 'Take it. It's yours now. And don't ever be scared again. Not of any thing nor any man. You understand?'

The boy nodded and his father reached out and handed him the medal and its case. As the boy turned to go the man said sharply, 'Boy.' And the boy turned. His father was smiling with the only side of his face that was capable of responding. He said softly, 'I'm proud of you, boy. Not that you killed the chicken but that you killed your own fear.'

Johnny Rennie gathered up just enough credits to get a university place. He took his Law finals twice and just passed on the second attempt. He got a half-blue for boxing and had a trial for the Scottish fifteen. He had two years with a firm of Edinburgh solicitors and was moderately successful but totally bored by what he saw as the fiddling detail of the law. It took too long to do so little and he felt it was on the side of the criminal rather than the victim. At the end of the two years he resigned from the practice and applied for a commission in the SAS.

But a commission in SAS has to be earned not applied for, and he reported at the depôt in Hereford as a private after three months' basic infantry training with the Black Watch. His toughness and tenacity were noted during his training and he was accepted as a sergeant at the end of the course. He was commissioned at the end of two years. His indifference to pain and his unquestioning loyalty and respect for his superiors were noted but there were some who worried that his attitude and personality bordered on the psychopathic. But the SAS psychologists found him normal enough and that was the end of the doubts.

When an unofficial request came through from the Ministry of Defence for an officer with certain qualifications that were not put in writing he had been offered the transfer to the Foreign Office and SIS. He had been interviewed by a number of people – long, testing interviews – and then he was re-trained and inducted into the service. Again there were doubts by some of his new masters but his unquestioning loyalty and courage gradually persuaded most of them that their fears were unfounded. SIS was more used to men who argued and debated than men who unquestioningly did what they were asked to do; and doubts or not, John Rennie was respected and highly valued by his immediate superiors.

Chapter 5

THE WROUGHT-IRON gate squealed on its hinges as Rennie went up the short garden path to the porch of what had once been his home, a Victorian semi in one of the leafy but dusty Chiswick streets beyond the tube station.

He pressed the bell and then stood back as if he were some door-to-door salesman trained to stand back to avoid looking aggressive.

She was wearing a bright red sweater and a black skirt that he hadn't seen before.

'You're early,' she said.

'On the dot actually, my dear. And how are you keeping?'

She ignored the question and stood aside so that he could enter the hallway. He stood there respectfully as she closed the front door and brushed past him, leading the way to the front living room.

He waited until she sat before sitting down himself. He wondered if it was accidental or something to do with Women's Lib that she chose to sit in 'his' old chair.

'How are the girls?'

'They're fine. They break up on Thursday. Their reports are on the table for you to see.'

'How have they done?'

She shrugged. 'Not bad. You may think otherwise.'

'Have you heard from Cowley?'

He saw her mouth go thin and pursed before she spoke.

'That's hardly your business now, Johnny. We *are* divorced if you remember.'

She was conscious of his brown eyes on her face. Those brown eyes that had always seemed to know what was going on in her mind. Except for that one solitary episode.

'You deserved better than him, my dear. He's a rascal.'

The old-fashioned word stuck in her mind. Cowley was a shit. A charming shit. Rascals belonged in Thomas Hardy novels. But it was typical of her ex-husband's vocabulary. She had wondered sometimes when it had happened if he wouldn't challenge Cowley to a duel. Pistols at dawn on Chiswick Common.

'Would you like a cup of tea?'

'Yes. I think I would. Very kind of you to offer.'

He sat reading the girls' school reports until she came back with a tray. As she put it down beside him he noticed that there was just one cup and a plate of biscuits.

He looked up at her. 'Elizabeth seems to be doing all right but young Mary seems to be resting on her laurels.'

'She's been a bit out of sorts recently. She'll make it up before long.'

'Out of sorts? What does that mean?'

She brushed a strand of blonde hair from her cheek as she looked at him. 'She's very fond of you. Johnny. They both are. But Mary's taken it all a bit to heart. She'll get over it. But it takes time.'

He stood up. And she knew that she had annoyed him. He didn't say so but she knew that for him she was the cause of any disturbance or unhappiness.

'I'd better be off,' he said brusquely. 'I'll call for them on Saturday at ten if that's agreeable to you. I'll have a little talk with Mary then.'

'You haven't had your tea.'

'See you on Saturday. I can see myself out.'

As Mary Rennie sat sewing buttons on to school dresses, glancing from time to time at the Wimbledon highlights, she wondered what kind of woman could have done better with John Hamish Rennie than she had done. Twelve years of marriage. Two of them in army married quarters. No great ups and downs. Not particularly boring. No problems of health or money. A straightforward, honest man who took his responsibilities seriously. Who was protective to

28

her and the girls. Polite to the point of punctiliousness. An opener of car doors. Decisive and self-confident, an ideal husband. All her friends said so, and there was no doubt that some of them envied her the quite handsome man who had put her on a pedestal.

She would never understand why she had got involved with Guy Cowley. He wasn't even her kind of man. And on reflection it wasn't even vaguely romantic. Sometimes she was almost ready to admit that it was nothing more than boredom with a husband who gave her no cause for complaint. But to admit that openly would cost her dignity. It was the behaviour of a wilful schoolgirl, not an adult woman.

Cowley had chatted her up in the supermarket. Carrying the heavy cardboard box with her groceries back to her car. Admiring her hair and her clothes, smiling that smooth, charming smile with the dimples and the cleft in the chin. He'd been there the next week, all too obviously waiting for her, laughing and unabashed when she had accused him. He had taken her for a mid-morning coffee at the White Hart. Somehow he had found out her name and where she lived and when he had phoned ten days later she had been too flustered just to hang up. He had invited himself round for a coffee. He had chatted amiably with the standard lacing of compliments and that had been all.

But gradually she came to look forward to the Friday encounters at Sainsbury's, and the coffee at the hotel. It was like meeting an old friend. She had kidded herself that it was romantic. A kind of rerun of *Brief Encounter*. But she had said nothing to her husband of the meetings and when Cowley had asked her if she had told her husband and she had said no she realised from the smile on his face that in that moment they had become fellow-conspirators. And he knew that too.

She knew that she was flattered by his interest, and by the end of three months of meetings it had seemed both inevitable and exciting when she had gone to his rooms by the bank one Friday morning. And half an hour later she was aware of a sense of pleasurable defiance of her husband as she lay naked on the bed with Cowley. Afterwards he

29

had talked vaguely of divorce and marriage and that had brought her down to earth. The thought of being with him permanently suddenly revolted her, and the thought of him with her two children seemed outrageous. She had never been back to Sainsbury's even now that she was divorced.

She had felt only a moment's surprise when her husband had confronted her. There are people whose mistakes and sins, no matter how small, are always inevitably exposed, and she was one of those people.

For the first time in her life she' had realised why her husband was so successful in his job. No anger, no abuse, just the continual calm probing. After her admission of the facts, the questions about motive. Why had she done it? Why that particular man? What were his attractions? Did she love the man? Did he love her? Was he going to stand by her once they were divorced? Her answers had been negative, and pathetic enough to have perhaps moved most other men. She told him that she had no complaints. No discontents. It had been an accident. A slow-motion nightmare like those TV action-replays of missed goals. She had always been aware of his almost ruthless attitude to the outside world, but with her and the girls he had always been different. Kind and considerate. But it was obvious that for him she was now part of that outside world and was to be treated accordingly.

He hadn't asked her if she wanted a divorce. For him it just flowed as a natural and automatic outcome of that single act of infidelity. He had expressed no sympathy for her, nor indignation or disappointment on his part. It was no more emotional than the ending of a business partnership, and strangely enough she had been carried along, even sustained, by that impersonal approach.

There had been no quarrel about financial things. The house remained his property but she was given a lifetime's lease at a peppercorn rent, and half his earnings went for her upkeep and that of the girls. He showed no embarrassment when he visited the house to pick up or deliver the girls and expressed no nostalgia or regret for old times.

And strangely enough the lack of emotion seemed to work out quite well with the two girls. It was almost as if he had not really ceased to be their father and her husband, but was merely away for even longer than in the days when they were married. He seemed to exert an influence on them all even when he wasn't there.

Just once, before the divorce finally went through, she had tentatively questioned his attitude. Was it really necessary for them to part? They could be at arm's length and uncommitted, but together for the girls' sake. It had been like arguing with a mathematician about the validity of the square on the hypotenuse. A vow had been made and the vow had been broken. With this particular kind of vow its breaching meant divorce. That was the law so far as Rennie was concerned. A simple straightforward formula. To question its inevitability was as pointless as trying to swim up Niagara Falls.

What seemed strange to her was that none of them appeared to have suffered unduly. His rigid attitude seemed to her to expunge her guilt, and life went on much as usual for all of them. She had asked him once if he ever thought of marrying again and it was obvious from his reactions that the thought had never entered his mind. Not that the answer was no, but just that he had never actually thought about it. He had frowned, shaken his head dismissively, and continued talking about the estimates for fixing the guttering on the conservatory.

She thought of him quite often and the image was always the same one. The rather handsome young man standing to attention in his best barathea uniform and polished Sam Browne, pale-blue parachute wings over the pocket. For her he always seemed to be standing to attention in uniform, even when he was wearing a sports jacket and slacks.

Chapter 6

THERE WAS a portrait of Disraeli on the panelled wall behind the long mahogany table, and through the half-open windows came the faint sounds of one of the Guards' regiments on their way to the Mall. The yelps of warrant officers' commands and the thud of the bass drum and the strains of 'Highland Laddie'.

The two men sat opposite each other at one end of the table. Fredericks in a black jacket and pin-stripes despite the heat, and Paynter in a light-weight two-piece. Fredericks had one of those pseudo-tired voices, the words precisely chosen but their definition diffused by the affected drawl. Despite the impression of casualness his eyes were alert and constantly observant. His manner he saw as a form of disguise. The casual drawl could give the impression that it represented what went on in that well-trained mind. It wasn't wise to let casual observers know one's real thoughts. It came to him naturally but had been refined by the daily contact with his Foreign Office colleagues. Fredericks was Foreign Office–SIS liaison, and Paynter was SIS, responsible for operations that were tactfully described as 'not conveniently fitting into the standard departmental hierarchy'. They had known one another for years and had been contemporaries at Oxford, Fredericks at Balliol and Paynter at St Anthony's. Normally when they met the atmosphere was civilised and relaxed but this day they were both subdued. It was Fredericks who broke the long silence.

'Have SDECE been cooperating?'

'It's hard to tell, Freddie. They haven't *done* anything but I don't think that's their fault. There's just nothing to go on. Except for the woman who thinks she saw him wave down a taxi nobody saw a thing.'

'Is there any significance in the fact that they called *Le Figaro* rather than *Le Monde*?'

'No. We're not even sure that they didn't call *Le Monde*. We daren't ask or it might come out in public.'

'And all they said was what?'

' "We've got Mason", and they gave the number on his ID card.'

'And it was said in French?'

'Yes. The voicé analysis said there were Turkish overtones, whatever that means.'

Fredericks sighed. 'If somebody has lifted him what does he know?'

'The usual mixed bag of operations. He's been on all sorts of things over the last five years. It depends on who's got him as to what he could give them that could be useful.'

'What was he actually doing in Paris?'

'Trying to patch things up with his wife. She'd started divorce proceedings against him.'

'On what grounds?'

'Incompatibility. Irretrievable breakdown of the marriage. Nothing spectacular.'

'Has anybody interviewed her?'

'No. We don't think she even knows he's not around. He wasn't staying with her, he'd taken a room for a couple of weeks.'

'Has his room been searched thoroughly?'

'No. We just asked the French for it to be sealed and that's what they've done. We didn't want to look too concerned.'

'Will the French keep it quiet?'

'I think they will. I asked my opposite number to put the lid on it. He was very cooperative. They don't like this sort of thing. They're not recognising officially that he's even a missing person.'

'Have you talked to the Turkish desk?'

'Yes. But without more information they can't help us. There are hundreds of dissident groups in Turkey. Could be any one of them. I don't want to go down that route until there's some real reason to.' He paused. 'Are the FO getting the wind-up?'

Fredericks shrugged. 'I'd say touchy rather than windy. But they're pros. They're used to the ups and downs.'

'Where will you be tonight?'

'At the Travellers until about seven and then at home.'

'Town or country home?'

Fredericks half-smiled. 'Town. Keep in touch no matter how little there is. If he's been lifted we'll hear from them before long. You'd better check whether we've got any political Turks in jail.'

'We have. Seven of the bastards. They're in the Scrubs. The governor would love to see the back of them.'

Fredericks looked across at Paynter. 'Do you ever get tired of all this, Hugo?'

'Of what, exactly?'

'The contrast. The smooth diplomats on the surface and the violence underneath it all.'

Paynter smiled. 'I sometimes wish I was a diplomat instead of what I am.'

'D'you think the public has any idea of what goes on in their name?'

'I don't imagine they think about it for a moment. They've got their mortgages to worry about.' He smiled. 'And the greenfly on the roses. Their kids' education and next year's holiday on the Algarve.'

Fredericks nodded. 'Sometimes when Angie is giving one of our routine dinner parties at the flat I look at them. Ambassadors and First Secretaries, MPs and visiting Senators and minor dictators, and I'm terribly tempted to say out loud what their governments are really doing. Financing dissidents to stir up trouble, training and arming assassins to murder some politician of a rival party or an unfriendly country. Infiltration to destabilise a whole country. And for what? A few years of power or money in a Swiss bank account. Tens, maybe hundreds of thousands of their countrymen killed or starving in some banana republic.

'And they sit there, Hugo, as smooth as they come. Babbling away about some resolution in the UN, how much they've just paid for half a dozen new suits, whether their wives or mistresses prefer Madame Rochas to Chanel Number Five and complaining that their illegally parked cars are towed away by the police. And all the time their minds are really on whether they should fund the IRA or the PLO or the latest group of Islamic lunatics. It doesn't seem credible. They're such bloody hypocrites. All of them. Us included.'

'Maybe you should come back into SIS, Freddie. There's no hypocrisy for us. We do the dirty deeds and that's the end of it. No philosophising.'

Fredericks looked towards the windows and sighed. 'Sometimes I'd like to leave it all and be a monk. In some silent order preferably.'

Paynter laughed softly and stood up. 'You'd always be arguing with the abbot. You need a holiday, Freddie. That's all that's the matter with you.'

There was no further information from Paris that night and Fredericks and Paynter met again in Fredericks's office at ten the following morning. Fredericks stood at the window and Paynter was aware of the handsome profile backlit from the sunshine outside. It was a Saturday and Fredericks had relaxed from the pin-stripes to a tweed suit. He looked every inch the actor that he had once aimed to be. For several minutes he was silent and then turned to look at Paynter.

'The Minister has been told. Wanted to know what SIS were doing about it. I told him there was nothing to go on. That it might even be a hoax. Suggested very, very diplomatically that the embassy could keep a watching brief on it.' Fredericks sighed. 'That caused an immediate eruption, and Carter was told to signal the ambassador and ensure that they showed no interest.

'I weaseled a bit and said that I only meant that the SIS staff at the embassy could nose around a little and that earned me a tirade about the shortcomings of SIS and the countless embarrassments that they caused to our embassies everywhere.' Fredericks shrugged and sighed. 'Why don't you send somebody over from here? Make it a sort of free-lance assignment. Never contacts the embassy and plays it very low-key.'

'I've already told someone to stand by.'

'Who?' Fredericks swung round to look at Paynter.

'John Rennie.'

Fredericks pursed his lips. 'Isn't there anybody else?'

'Not who's suitable. You've never given Rennie his due. Why don't you?'

'God knows. I can't put my finger on it . . .'

'There must be something.'

'He's such a zombie, Hugo.'

'What's that mean in Foreign Office semantics these days?'

'Inflexible. Unimaginative. And a thug.'

Paynter smiled wryly 'For inflexible read patriotic, for unimaginative read loyal, and for thug . . .' He shrugged. 'Well, it's thugs he has to deal with most of the time. We don't intend sending lambs to the slaughter if that's what you want.'

'But he's so right-wing you could justifiably say that he's a Fascist.'

Paytner laughed. 'Nonsense. Rennie isn't the slightest bit interested in any kind of politics. Not even vaguely . . .' He paused. 'We've all sworn and signed to protect Queen and Country from their enemies . . . the only thing you don't like about him is that unlike the rest of us he actually means it. Every word of it. No dodging. No interpreting. The Queen's commission and all that.'

'But he's so bloody naïve.'

'He's not, actually. He's just loyal. Maybe a bit too black and white in his judgements but he's utterly dependable. And that's more than you can say for some of your Foreign Office friends.'

'Oh God. Don't let's go over Burgess and Maclean and all that *galère* again.'

'I don't mean them. I mean some of your contemporaries. Very sophisticated. Very intellectual. And I wouldn't trust them an inch.'

Fredericks smiled and said quietly, 'You're right of

course. We're just swapping prejudices. I guess what I'm looking for doesn't exist.'

Paynter shrugged. 'If they've got complex, searching minds they'll never be totally committed. Rennie's a bit Beau Geste and the Union Jack and all that, but he knows what he's doing and he does it well. Don't let's beat him over the head with his virtues. We need 'em. I wish I'd got more like him. I'd sleep a lot better of nights.'

'I ought not to comment. It's not my business.' Fredericks half-smiled. 'What a funny world. I'm getting more stick-in-the-mud every day. When did it all start getting out of hand? It used not to be like this.'

'I think it started when they killed Jack Kennedy. It was like some kind of signal that if that was possible then anything was possible. It was a sort of bench-mark.'

Fredericks nodded. 'As Antony said, "Cry 'Havoc!' and let slip the dogs of war".' He paused and grimaced. 'Let's have a drink. What do you want, Glenlivet or Jamieson Ten Year Old?'

'Jamieson's, but no water or soda, thanks.'

Chapter 7

PAYNTER HAD allocated Rennie an office, and after his briefing, Rennie sat at the small table reading Mason's file, his sports jacket draped over the back of the issue chair, his shirt sleeves rolled up.

Most SIS field agents would have complained at being assigned to such a wild-goose chase, but Rennie took it as a compliment to his abilities. And in a way it was.

Mason was 42, married to a French girl of 26. He had been on assignments in Hong Kong, Brazil, Sydney, Johannesburg, and Addis Ababa in the last five years. He had not been to Turkey either on duty or holiday and the only Arab country he had been to was a brief three-day visit to Cairo eight years ago. And that was only for a routine check on the embassy security system.

The brief notes on Mason's marital troubles he found interesting. Mason didn't speak good French and when he was away his young wife paid visits to Paris and had been seen with several different men in nightclubs and discos. Mason had not been officially told that his wife was under surveillance but somebody had obviously tipped him off. There was an unsubstantiated suggestion that he had reacted violently. Then there had been a series of reconciliations and more quarrels. The girl had no criminal or subversive connections and it looked as if her behaviour was a mixture of genuine loneliness and an incipient promiscuity. She had started the divorce action in London as that was their technical domicile and she was now a British subject, which she apparently resented.

Rennie found it difficult to understand how a man could want to be reconciled with a woman who behaved like that.

Why did he wait for her to divorce him? Why didn't he just walk right out and divorce her? They had made a mutual promise, a contract even, and the woman had broken the contract. What use was that kind of woman to a man?

He knew Harry Mason reasonably well. He had great charm and some of his work had been brilliant. But there must be a flaw in his character somewhere. Maybe it was that flaw that had got him into this mess. And it may be that the mess was part of his private life and nothing to do with his SIS work. But in that case why the cryptic telephone call to the French newspaper? And why did they quote his field identity number?

Rennie closed the file and spoke to Paynter's secretary on the internal phone. Paynter could see him right away.

Paynter finished talking and put down the phone and looked questioningly at Rennie.

'I've read the file, Hugo.'

'What did you think of it?'

'It's either something connected with his private life or it's something bigger than it looks.'

'Well, whichever it is we've got to find him. Are you planning to go over to Paris?'

'I don't think it will do much good but I planned to go tomorrow if you can lay on funds, tickets and facilities in time.'

'I'll tell Harris to get you whatever you want.' Paynter stood up to end the interview. 'Keep me in touch.'

'I'll be taking a transceiver and I'll leave a schedule with Signals so you can contact me too.'

'Take care.'

Rennie smiled as he left, but said nothing.

The SDECE man helped him carry his kit up the creaking wooden stairs, and on the top landing Rennie waited as the Frenchman broke the official seal and unlocked the heavy padlock that had been temporarily fixed to the door. Almost ceremoniously he handed Rennie the normal door-key as if it absolved him from any further involvement in the British problem. Rennie invited him inside but the Frenchman pleaded urgent work waiting for him back at his office.

It was one large room and the air was stale and still. There was a divan against the wall in the far corner. An old-fashioned wardrobe, a chest of drawers, a table with a plastic top and two tubular chairs. Facing the door was a curtain on a curved rail that marked off the kitchen which consisted of a small, chipped enamel sink, a draining-board and a box turned on its end that had a few cloths and bottles on its centre shelf. Two empty jam jars held a small clutter of cutlery and on the shelves of a crudely-made, open, triangular, corner-cupboard there were a few packets and tins and a cheap combined tin- and bottle-opener.

Rennie unpacked one of his bags and took out the leather case that housed the transceiver. He had to reset the voltage wheel before he slid the plug into the travel convertor plug that fitted the two-pin socket by the bed. He pressed the buttons and watched as the LEDs ran through the frequencies until he found the one he wanted. He pressed the memory button and then tuned the night-time frequency and entered that in the memory too. He looked at his watch. There were five minutes to go until the scheduled time. 1300 hours GMT, plus the date in minutes, and 2300 hours GMT with the same addition.

He switched on and turned the switch to 'Receive' and the blips came through at half-volume. He turned the volume down and left the radio warming up. Its micro-circuitry needed no warming up as the older equipment did, but it was a habit that was hard to break.

London acknowledged dead on time and he tapped out his location on the built-in key. When the radio was back in its case he looked around for somewhere to conceal it. There was nowhere suitable and in the end he edged the divan away from the wall and placed the radio in the corner angle and shoved the divan back against the wall.

He knew that despite its bareness he would have to search the room, but its depressing stillness tempted him to go out first for a meal or a snack. He looked at his watch. It was twenty minutes to midnight. He was not a man to succumb to temptation.

Rennie carried out the search as if it were a demonstration of technique on an agents' course. Two hours later he looked at the small display of the fruits of his search laid out on the plastic table. One thing was certain, they gave no clues to what had happened although they were indications that Mason had actually used the room. But that had never really been in doubt. He had paid for the room in his own name, and had given the address to the SIS man based at the embassy.

There was a crumpled gold pack of Stuyvesants with two cigarettes still inside it. A parking ticket for the long-stay carpark at Heathrow. A ball-point pen that was sticky as if it had been used to stir a cup of coffee or tea. A 10p coin and two blank pages ripped from a diary for that year and the month of May.

Rennie ignored his hunger, undressed slowly and lay on the creaking divan bed. He slept soundly until seven the next morning.

Mason's room was in the 10ème in an old house in a back street near the Gare du Nord, and Rennie took a taxi to the address near the Metro station St Philippe du Roule.

There were geraniums in clay pots on the steps up to the door and the front door was open. The card under the top bell said 'Mme Mason'. He walked up to the third floor and pushed the well-polished brass bell. It was a couple of minutes before she opened the door. She looked younger than her 26 years. Blonde and pretty, and frail-looking in a pale blue peignoir embroidered with dark blue irises.

'Mrs Mason?'

'Who are you?' She spoke with only a trace of a French accent.

'I'm a colleague of your husband, Mrs Mason. Could I speak to you for a few moments?'

'There's no point. I won't change my mind. I told Harry that.'

'It's not about your domestic problems, Mrs Mason.'

42

'I don't understand.'

'I'm trying to contact him. I think you could help.'

For a moment she hesitated and then she opened the door wider and stood aside to let him in. The room was spacious and the furnishings elegant. Plain white walls and polished wood floors. She pointed to a comfortable armchair. 'Do sit down please.' She looked at him, curiosity in her eyes. 'What is it you want?'

'My name's Rennie, Mrs Mason, John Rennie. As I said, I'm a colleague of Harry's and I'm trying to contact him.'

'He doesn't live here,' she said quietly. 'He's got a room somewhere near the Gare du Nord.'

'Yes. I've been there but he's not there.'

'Maybe he was asleep or shopping or something.'

'When did you see him last?'

'It was nearly two weeks ago.'

'Did he seem OK?'

She sighed. 'Do you know him well?'

'I used to know him well. I haven't seen him for a couple of years.'

'He was upset because of our situation.'

'The divorce proceedings?'

'Yes.'

'How upset was he?'

She looked towards the window for a few seconds and then back at Rennie. 'He was very upset.' She paused. 'You said you were a colleague of his. Does that mean you do the same kind of work that he does?'

'Tell me what you think he does.'

'He always says he works for the Foreign Office. The English Foreign Office, but I think it is more than that.'

'In what way more?'

'I think he did secret work. Like the SDECE here in France.'

'What makes you think that?'

'He was always leaving me. Going off suddenly. Sometimes I didn't hear from him for weeks. He brought me back things from foreign places. He was away more than he was with me. And when he confronted me about going out with other men it was obvious that I had been watched very carefully. He knew so much.'

'Was he violent towards you?'

'Only the first time, and when I told him of the divorce. Then he threatened me.'

'What did he threaten you with?'

'He said he would kill me if I left him.'

'Did you believe that?'

'Half I believed it.'

'Are you scared of him?'

'Yes.' She said it calmly, as if it needed no explanation.

'Did you mention the threat to any of your men friends?' She shook her head and he knew she was lying, but he let it go.

'Would you mind telling me why you wanted a divorce?'

She shrugged. 'He put his job before me. He left me alone for weeks on end. I was lonely so I went out with other people.'

'What kind of man was your husband?'

'Maybe you know better than I do.'

'Tell me what you think.'

'He was attractive . . . and charming . . . but he didn't understand. He said I was a whore . . . he didn't understand that I was so lonely.'

'But you don't have to sleep with a man just because he takes you out.'

She shrugged. 'In Paris you do. I think in London is the same.'

'Maybe Harry was lonely too. Wishing he was with you.'

'He could have changed his job and been with me every day. He preferred his job to me.'

'In our kind of job we have no choice but to go off at a moment's notice. We can't tell our wives or friends where we are going or what we are doing. They would be put in danger if they were told. And other people's lives can depend on a quick response when it's needed. It isn't just Harry.'

'He could have got another job. He's got a degree.'

'It's not just a job, Mrs Mason. It's more a calling. A bit like a priest, I suppose.'

'Maybe. But priests don't marry.'

'Do you expect to see Harry again soon?'

'No. I told him not to come back again. And my solicitor had sent him a letter to say that he shouldn't pester me.'

'Can you remember the last thing he said to you?'

'Yes Very well. He was standing outside the door here and he said I was a whore but he loved me. He was crying.'

'Can I ask you one more question?'

'Yes.'

'The men you went around with. Were they all Frenchmen?'

'All except one.'

'What nationality was he?'

'He was an Arab but I don't know which Arab country he came from.'

'Can you remember his name?'

'His first name was Khalim. I don't know his other name.'

'What was he like? Was he a tough sort of fellow?'

She smiled. 'No. He was charming. Very attractive. Very wealthy and he was here on a visit. Not at all tough. He was well-educated. I think he had been to Cambridge or Oxford. He spoke perfect English and French.'

Rennie stood up. He was almost certain that he had wasted his time. 'It was very kind of you to speak to me, Mrs Mason. I hope things work out for you and Harry one way or another.'

Rennie didn't wait for the radio schedule but used the scrambler at the embassy to phone London and ask for copies of the surveillance reports on Mason's wife to be sent over. They arrived in the evening diplomatic bag and Humphries, SIS's man based at the embassy, brought them to his room.

As he poured Humphries a whisky from his duty-free bottle he said, 'Who did the surveillance on Mrs Mason?'

Humphries shrugged. 'I did most of it. A new guy from London did the rest. Phillips I think his name was.'

'When was all this done?'

'Eight, nine months ago roughly. I don't remember. It didn't have any priority.'

'Who initiated it?'

'Paynter. He was worried about a wife getting mixed up with the wrong people.'

'Was she?'

'Was she what?'

'Getting mixed up with undesirables?'

'They were the usual Paris creeps. Her family's got plenty of money. And she was opening her legs for most of them. They weren't political, if that's what you mean. Just socialites. The French equivalent of Sloane Rangers, but older.'

'Were they all French?'

'So far as I can remember.'

'I thought there was an Arab as well.'

'Not that I came across anyway.'

'Did you know Mason?'

'I met him several times.'

'What did you think of him?'

'He was OK. A bit . . . I don't know the word . . . a bit undecided. No . . . it was more than that. A bit uncommitted. He was crazy about that two-timing wife of his and I think that put him off his stroke most of the time.'

'What kind of places did these guys take her to?'

'Oh God. From four star to the gutter. London raised hell about my expenses. I sometimes had to use locals, in some of the places I would have been recognised. Some were the best in town but most of them were dives.'

'I may want to look over one or two. Could you spare the time to come with me? My French is terrible.'

'I'm OK for the next week but after that we've got a security audit at the embassy and I'll be on the hop all the time.'

'I'll phone you tomorrow morning. Another drink?'

'No thanks. I'll get back and close down.'

Rennie spent the evening reading the surveillance reports and noting the places and, when they were identified, the names of the men Mrs Mason had been seen with.

He and Humphries had visited six of the places over two nights and Humphries had had long boozy chats with bartenders, trying to find out if they had ever heard of a wealthy man named Khalim. There had been no response. Nightclub bartenders don't talk indiscreetly about their patrons even if they know their identities.

They were sitting in a dingy club in a side-street off the Boulevard des Capucines. The music was deafening and the flashing lights were almost hypnotic as they sat finishing their drinks, shaking their heads amiably but decisively at a succession of girls who came to their table.

'There's one other way, you know, Humphries.'

'What's that?'

'The Immigration people will have records of foreigners entering the country. She said the Arab was just visiting. Could you get a look at the records for this period? Just the visitors from Arab countries. They're probably categorised so that they can be passed to SDECE.'

'I don't have any contact with Immigration. The embassy's bound to. But they'll be very sticky. They like to pretend I don't exist.'

'How about the Deuxième Bureau?'

'I'd stand a better chance there. Especially if I could offer a trade.'

'See what you can do tomorrow.'

'OK. I'll try.'

Humphries was waiting outside Mason's room when Rennie got back from lunch.

'Any luck?'

'I think so. I've made some notes.'

Rennie unlocked the door and waved Humphries inside. As they sat at the tatty table Humphries pulled a folded sheet of paper from his inside pocket. 'They wouldn't co-operate unless I told them the name I was looking for. Said they wouldn't cooperate if it was just a fishing expedition. I gave them a description. What Mason's wife had told you. Wealthy, handsome and all that and when I said his first name was Khalim they said they knew who I meant.'

'Well done. Tell me what you've got.'

Humphries unfolded the paper and read from his notes.

'Khalim Abu Said. Forty-three years old. Born in Jerusalem. Now living in Amsterdam. Describes himself as a merchant. Net worth unknown but certainly a multimillionaire. Was at Oxford, Balliol, and two years at the London School of Economics. Firsts in everything and played tennis for his college. Married with two children. A boy and a girl. Has some sort of diplomatic status as semi-official consul for several Arab states. Including Libya. Has diplomatic passports for Saudi Arabia and . . . believe it or not . . . the USA.' Humphries looked up at Rennie. 'That's about it, Johnny. Hope it's enough.'

'It's a good lead. Thanks. Did they squeeze you for anything?'

'No. Not a thing. I've got the feeling they knew why we were looking for Khalim Said.'

'What makes you think they knew?'

'When I was leaving the guy smiled and said, "Let us know what happens." '

Rennie said, 'Thanks for your help. I'll be leaving tomorrow.'

The phone rang for a long time before Fleur Mason answered. He'd asked for just ten minutes of her time and very reluctantly she'd agreed to see him at six that evening.

She was wearing a vivid green dress and he was aware of her beautiful neck and shoulders as he noticed the pearls she was wearing. When they were both seated he said, 'The other day you told me that your husband threatened to kill you if you left him. Did you really believe him?'

She looked down at the ring on her finger before she replied. 'As a man I didn't think that he would kill me. Not even in his anger and depression. But because of his work I wondered if I might be mistaken.'

'Do you still have any affection for him?'

For several moments she closed her eyes, thinking. Then she said slowly, 'Affection, yes. Love, no. He was a very nice man in many ways. Like I said, it was his job and the leaving me was the problem.'

'Would you be upset if something happened to him?'

'I don't understand. Is he ill?'

'No. But I think he might be in some danger.'

'From to do with his job?'

'Possibly. I'm trying to find out. I very much need your help.'

'How on earth can I help?' Her shrug was very French.

'Would you answer me two questions absolutely truthfully? Personal questions.'

'Of course.'

'The Arab you mentioned, Khalim. Did you sleep with him?'

It was several seconds before she said softly, 'Yes, I slept with him twice.'

'Did you talk about your husband and the divorce?'

'Only in passing.' She shrugged. 'He asked if I was married and I told him of the divorce.'

'Did you tell him why you were divorcing Harry?'

'A little.'

'Please tell me. It's very important.'

She shrugged. 'I told him the facts. The truth.'

'What did he say?'

'He seemed sympathetic to Harry. Said that men in that kind of work had to make sacrifices for their cause, for their country.'

'Did he ask any more about Harry's job?'

'Just how long he does it. Where we lived in London. Just gossip. I don't remember. It didn't seem important.'

'Did Khalim say where he lived?'

'No. But he said he was just a visitor to Paris.'

'He hasn't contacted you since?'

'No.'

Rennie stood up. 'Thanks for your help. I won't trouble you again.'

She stood up and walked with him to the door. As he opened it she said, 'What has happened to him, to Harry?'

'I don't know. Maybe nothing. Don't worry.'

He was conscious of her standing at the door, watching him as he clattered down the stairs.

Chapter 8

THE REPORTS had come back in 24 hours from the SIS stations in Damascus, Teheran, Baghdad, Riyadh and Cairo, but there was nothing. Khalim Abu Said was exactly what he appeared to be, a millionaire several times over, an acceptable person in most Arab states and he had semi-diplomatic status. And he had no known connection with terrorist groups. There was no reliable SIS source of information in Tripoli and no request had been put to the SIS people in Holland.

Paynter was edgy and doubtful. 'There's nothing to go on, Johnny. His only connection is that he slept with Mason's wife.'

'And he asked about Mason's job.'

'That could be just the usual flannel. Trying to look interested in the girl before he got her into bed.'

'Or confirming what he already knew about Mason.'

'I think you're just clutching at straws.'

'He's the only straw we've got.'

'And that's about all there is to make him interesting. For me it's not really enough.' Paynter paused. 'Why are you so keen?'

'Just instinct and experience.'

'Let's wait a couple more days. If we don't hear anything by then you can go over and check him out. At least he'd be eliminated.' He sighed. 'I'm just wondering if we aren't off on a wild-goose chase and Mason's just gone off somewhere to lick his marital wounds. Where are you going to be over the rest of the weekend?'

'I'll be at the flat. The girls are with me for the weekend.'

'I'll contact you if anything comes in. Collins in admin

wants to see you to go over your Paris expenses. But leave that until Monday if you want.'

Collins was an old hand and not unnecessarily tough with field agents' expenses unless they tried it on. He usually accepted Rennie's expenses without reference to him but as Rennie sat down Collins said, 'There's no way I can apportion these expenses, Johnny. You haven't given an indication of what they're for.'

Rennie shrugged. 'Just put it down as routine surveillance.'

'What? Nearly five hundred quid in six days.'

'I've spent five hundred quid in an hour before now.'

'Sure. But for a specific operation. What the hell was this?'

'Ask Paynter.'

'Why all the mystery? Just give me a code name. I don't need to know what it was about.'

'Just ask Paynter. He'll give you something. We just don't want anything on the record. Not yet anyway.'

Collins shrugged and sighed his exasperation. 'I'll put it down to the embassy audit. They won't notice.'

There were only two bedrooms in Rennie's flat and the two girls had to sleep in the same bed which, with the perversity of children, they loved.

'It's time, girls. Get undressed and I'll come in and say goodnight.'

'Will you read to us. Just a little bit?'

It was Mary who smiled as she asked, her head to one side, her brown eyes on his face.

'If you're quick I will. Don't forget to do your teeth.'

'I forgot my toothbrush, daddy. Can I use yours?'

He looked at the small girl. They were so different from one another. Elizabeth meticulous and tidy and already a bit of a loner. And the little one, Mary, eager and excitable, desperately untidy but equally desperately loving and affectionate.

52

'No,' he said. 'That's unhygienic. Give them an extra clean when you get back home.'

As he washed up the tea things he could hear the normal laughing and shouting that went with bed-times when they were with him. It seemed strange to him. Their mother was mild and vague but they never messed about when it was bed-time at home. But with him, the disciplinarian, they seemed always to have known that they could get away with it. Then they were calling that they were ready. As he sat on the bed he said, 'Who's going to choose?'

Mary sat up quickly. 'It's my turn.'

'What do you want, sweetie?'

'I want . . . I want . . . "Bed in Summer" by Robert Louis Stevenson. The book's on the little table there.'

He reached for the book, found the poem and read it to them. Then he closed the book. As he leaned forward to kiss the little one she said, 'Beth told me to ask you something.'

He leaned back looking at Elizabeth. 'Why don't you ask me yourself?'

She blushed and Mary said, 'She was scared to. She said you wouldn't be cross if I asked you.'

He shrugged. 'OK. Ask me.'

The small voice said, 'Why aren't you at home with us any more? We miss you.' She looked at her sister. 'We both do, don't we, Beth?' Her sister nodded vigorously.

'What did your mother tell you?'

'She just said you'd had a disagreement and to ask you if we wanted to know more.'

Rennie hesitated and then he was back in his normal skin again. He said matter-of-factly, 'When people get married they make some promises. Your mother didn't keep one of them.'

'Momma always keeps her promises.' Elizabeth's face was red with embarrassment and challenge. 'She's a very nice mother.'

Rennie nodded. 'Of course she is. The very best. Anyway. . . . .Don't worry about us. We're OK. And we both love you. All the love there is.'

He kissed them both and left the door half open so that

they could see the light from the hall.

He switched on the TV and poured himself a drink, changing channels to the ITV news before he sat down. He didn't absorb what was on the screen. He was trying to think what better answer he could have given. He had told the truth but it wasn't enough. And the whole truth was not for children. Maybe the whole truth wasn't for anybody. As with his work, the public didn't need to know about the things that had to be done to protect them.

They spent the Sunday morning at the Zoo and when it started to rain he took them in a taxi to the Science Museum and the Natural History Museum. Then tea at the hotel in Sloane Square.

When they arrived back at their home he told the taxi-driver to wait and walked up the path to the door. She had seen them arrive and was standing at the open door.

'Johnny. A man phoned. He said he'd been trying to contact you. Would you ring him right away.'

'What's his name?'

'I think it was Payne or Paynter. I've written it out and his telephone number. It's on the pad by the telephone.'

'Do you mind if I use your phone?'

'Of course not. Do you want to pay off the taxi?'

'I'll see what Paynter wants. I might need the taxi.'

There was barely one ring before the phone was lifted at the other end.

'Hugo Paynter speaking.'

'It's Johnny, Hugo. I got your message to phone you.'

'They've been in touch, Johnny. They've got him. They even knew my unlisted phone number.'

'Who are they?'

'Can you come round to my place now?'

'Yes. I'll be there in about fifteen minutes.'

'I'll be waiting for you.'

Paynter's man, Wharton, answered his ring. An ex-Hong Kong policeman, his expressionless eyes looked over

Rennie and then he stood aside, and as Rennie walked in Paynter appeared in a faded but elegant denim safari suit.

'Ah, Johnny. Let's go upstairs to my study.'

Paynter poured them each a whisky and sat down facing Rennie.

'They phoned me here. A local call from a pay-phone. It looks like you could be right. They said they'd got Mason.' He paused and said softly. 'They want us to release four men we've got in jail. The men are all Arabs. Known terrorists. Not yet been brought before the courts. They've given us two weeks to agree a deal.'

'Did they say who they were?'

'Yes. He said he was speaking on behalf of . . .' He looked at his notes. *El Jihad el Islami,* an Iranian group sponsored by the ayatollahs. It means "The holy Islamic war".'

'Why do they give us so long? Fourteen days. Kidnappers usually want a decision inside a couple of days.'

'They want something else apart from the release of the terrorists. In fact I'm not sure that they're all that interested in us releasing their mates.'

'What else do they want?'

Paynter sighed and leaned back in his chair. 'Seems that they've got hold of some Israeli equipment. They don't know how to use it. They want us to train them.'

'What kind of equipment?'

Paynter looked at his notes again. 'It's all electronic surveillance equipment. Battlefield stuff. Jamming equipment. Intercept equipment. But their main problem is a remotely piloted plane. Israeli made, called Mastiff. It's not the latest Israeli RPV but it could be useful to the PLO.'

'Are these people PLO?'

'No. But I'd guess that they're probably backed by the Syrians who control what's left of the PLO. We don't have much on them on the files. But they sound like a mixed bunch of thugs from Syria, Iran, and Libya, being used by Islamic fanatics.'

'Can we do what they want?'

'Yes. But if the Israelis found out that we'd been training Arab terrorists to use Israeli equipment against them they'd raise hell all over the place. Including Washington.'

'And if we don't do what they want, they bury Mason.'

Paynter shook his head. 'No. More than that in a way. Apparently they've made Mason write out a description of all his assignments over the last five years. If we don't play ball it'll be sent to the press. Here, Europe and the States.'

'So we just deny them. Say they're fakes. Hitler's Diaries stuff.'

'Not if they've still got Mason. They could offer the press interviews with him.'

'So what have the brass decided?'

'We'll play ball. At least it's going to take time that we can be using for our own purposes. The equipment isn't British-made. We need to check what information we have. We'd have to go to wherever it's being kept, and that's probably in the Lebanon. And we need to check it over before it can be used. We can spin the time out for weeks.'

'How do we contact these people?'

'The usual story. Don't phone us we'll phone you. There's one other thing. I phoned Lambert in Amsterdam. He phoned me back about an hour ago. We had to talk in parables but the long and short of it is that your friend Khalim Said was reported to have been in Teheran a month ago. He went to Damascus on the way back.'

'Have you put Lambert in the picture?'

'No. I haven't told him anything. I want you to deal with it.'

'Why not Lambert?'

'For several reasons. Lambert doesn't come under me. Secondly he's a desk type not a . . .' he hesitated. '. . . not one of us. And thirdly Mason's one of my men. It's up to us to get him out.'

'Are these people going to leak it to the media?'

'No. They threatened to kill Mason if we told the press.'

'Why should they do that? They usually love the publicity. That's half the reason why they bomb and kill.'

'I'd say they want that equipment in service for some operation that's only in the planning stage.'

'What do you want me to do?'

Paynter shrugged. 'I want you to find out where they're holding him and get him back.'

'What resources do I get?'

'Anything you want. Within reason money no object. Men and equipment. Say what you want and it's yours. But until you know more, keep it very low-key. When you have to move then be as discreet as you can short of risking losing him. We don't want anyone to get even a faint whiff of what's going on. I've alerted Facilities already. They're standing by. I've told them to lay on dollars and guilders for tonight if necessary.'

'I'll need to do some background checking before I go over.'

'Where will you start?'

'With Khalim Said.'

'Do your best for us, Johnny.'

Rennie just smiled and nodded as he stood up. But he was well aware of the extra courtesy of his boss when he escorted him down to the front door himself.

Rennie spent the night at his office making notes of the basics that he would need. Paynter saw him at ten o'clock, marking his cooperation by walking through to Rennie's office. He pulled out a chair and sat opposite him.

'You look done in, Johnny. How much sleep did you get?'

'None. I'll sleep while you're looking into what I need in Amsterdam.'

'OK. Tell me.'

'I want a twenty-four-hour radio network. A system that covers voice and CW.'

'Do you want an operator for CW?'

'It would help.'

'OK.'

'I want an introduction to somebody, preferably a woman, who mixes in Khalim Said's set. A way in to him. She doesn't need to know anything about the operation.'

'Not easy. I'll see what pressure we can put on the embassy to cooperate.'

'I want a really sound cover. Something that will stand up to a check.'

'No problem.'

'I want surveillance equipment and an operator. I want him to check that I'm not bugged as well. I want a guy who can get through electronic security, and I want weapons. A PPK for me, with silencer. Machine pistols, say four, and maybe more later on. I'll let you know.

'I want credit references with two different Dutch banks and money available in four banks, one British. And I want a personal contact in Amsterdam, round the clock. Messages, maybe help, and no questions asked.'

'I'll get people working on it.' Paynter held out his hand. 'Let me have your notes as a check. Get some sleep and contact me when you're ready. My girl will know where I am. I'll tell her to give you top priority.'

'I want time to see my girls before I go.'

Paynter looked blank. 'Girls? – ah yes – your daughters. Of course. I'm sure you can manage that. And on family things, if you get over here a time or two you might grab me some of that lovely Dutch asparagus. There's a place at Schiphol that sells it. Wonderful stuff.'

Chapter 9

RENNIE TOOK the early B-Cal flight to Amsterdam and at Schiphol he hung around until all the other passengers on the flight had passed through immigration and collected their baggage from the conveyor. His two bags were the only ones left still circling on the belt. He took a taxi to de Bijenkorf and when it had gone he carried his bags across to the Krasnapolsky and booked in for a week.

It took him two days to find what he wanted and at the real-estate office on the Damrak he paid three months' rental in advance on the apartment on the Prinsengracht.

There was a large living room, one double bedroom and a single bedroom. The kitchen and bathroom were modern and well fitted out. The furnishings of the rooms were better than he had expected. It was owned by a Dutch diplomat who was working at the UN in New York. He spent a morning rigging the radio in the smaller bedroom, and tested out the network to London. He decided that he could get by in the first few days without a radio operator.

In every city where Rennie had ever operated there was always one man he could call on for information and help. They were never diplomats, and seldom British. More often than not they were criminals. Swaggering, arrogant, ruthless men with a network of information on places and people, able to carry out surveillance and act as go-betweens and lead him to any kind of specialist from forgery to burglary. They knew more about the secrets of their cities than its government and police. The man he hoped to find in Amsterdam was Jan Branders.

He checked through the telephone directory but there was no entry for Jan Branders. Plenty of Branders but not the kind of addresses where Jan would hang out. Jan Branders had been one of his informers in Surinam before the military coup in 1980. A pale-brown Creole, he had been totally reliable for the few months that Rennie had been there and it was Rennie and SIS who had helped him escape to Holland when the sergeants took over. A hundred thousand Surinamese had fled the small country just before independence in 1975 but Jan Branders would never have made it on his own. The military had offered a tempting reward for his capture. He had been an officer of the band of several hundred mercenaries who had invaded Surinam from French Guiana to liberate the country. Only Jan Branders and five others escaped capture. Like all Surinamese he had been a Dutch national before independence and Rennie had heard that he was now part of the underworld that controlled the girls and drugs over the small bridge from the Damrak. And that was where he'd have to look for him.

The houses and buildings of the red-light district of Amsterdam are as old and historic as the rest of the city, and despite the ruthlessness of the men who control it the area has a kind of innocence despite its activities. The girls sitting bathed in the purple or orange lights in the windows catered for every taste. A few were young and pretty, most were bored-looking and in their thirties, and a few were stout motherly figures whose attractions would appeal only to the most Freudian tastes.

It was almost ten o'clock as Rennie wended his way through the narrow alleyways to the canals. There was a small coffeeshop between two sex cinemas and Rennie sat at the counter aware of the eyes that watched him from the other tables, from the men lounging as lookouts at the open door, and from the cobbled street. Outsiders were not welcome. They belonged in the cobbled streets, browsing in sex-shops or staring at the girls. The coffeeshop was for locals and they resented any intrusion. The chatter went on in half a dozen languages, none of them Dutch.

When he ordered a second coffee the coloured man behind the counter said quietly, 'You Engelse?'

Rennie smiled and nodded. 'I'm looking for a friend.'

The man didn't look up as he filled Rennie's cup. 'Is plenty friends in the windows.'

Rennie paused over a five-guilder note. 'I'm looking for Jan Blanders.'

'Who he?' the man said without interest.

'An old friend of mine.'

The man pushed over his coffee and the change from the note.

'Keep the change.'

The man left the coins lying there and walked over to speak to a group of three men at the table in the corner. Five minutes later a man got onto the stool next to him. The man behind the counter handed him a cafe-filtre in a metal holder without being asked. The man's dark skin was pock-marked and the pale line of a knife scar ran from the side of his mouth to behind his ear. Without looking at Rennie he said, 'What you want, mijnheer – smack?'

Rennie turned to look at his face. The eyes were black, the whites laced with blood vessels. 'I'm looking for a friend.'

'Who the friend, man?'

'His name's Jan Branders.'

'Why you look here?'

'He lives in this area.'

'Who say he lives here.'

Rennie said, smiling. 'I do.' And without turning Rennie was aware of a man moving onto the stool on the other side of him. And a voice said, 'You come outside now, mister.'

Rennie shook his head and a big brown hand closed on his upper arm. He looked at the second man's face. He was white, bald at the front but not more than twenty-five or six with a round pudding face and a rash of raw spots that were oozing yellow pus. As Rennie looked at him he clamped his hand over the man's fingers on his arm and squeezed them tightly together, his thumb holding them flat so that the bones crushed together. In the cracked mirror behind the bar he saw a third man move up behind him, and a voice said softly, '*He, hoe maak jy het, Johnny?*' As he turned the voice said something in Dutch and the men on either side of him moved away. And Jan Branders moved onto

61

one of the empty stools.

He was smiling as he said, 'What in hell you doing here?'

Rennie looked back without smiling. 'Looking for you. Why the gorillas?'

'Gorillas? What is gorillas?'

'The two apes sitting each side of me.'

'Oh them?' he smiled. 'They friends of mine. They think maybe you from narcotics squad. What they call it? – *agent provocateur?*'

'Where can we talk?'

'Is OK here?'

'Not for me. Where can we go?'

'What is about?'

'Money. Information.'

Jan Branders smiled. 'Money OK. Information forgetting.' He paused. 'You know Jewish Historical Museum by Nieuw Markt?'

'I can find it.'

'OK. I meet you there in ten minutes, yes?'

'OK.'

The coffeeshop had been almost silent as they talked, and the chatter started again as Rennie went up the steps to the door.

As he walked across the bridges and through to the Gelderskade he was glad to be one of the crowd again. But as he turned right towards the museum the crowds thinned and the groups in the shop entrances were Surinamese and Javanese, and a few Chinese in the small shops that were still open.

He walked slowly round the museum building and finally stood between two parked cars. He saw Jan Branders walking across the square towards him, his hands in his jacket pockets. It wasn't the kind of welcome he had expected. Then Branders was standing in front of him staring at his face.

'You look younger, Johnny.'

Rennie shrugged. 'And you look older. Why the Mafia welcome?'

'You picked one of the drug places to have your coffee. That's where all the big deals are done. You were lucky you

62

asked for me so soon. They usually throw strangers in the canal. The police don't interfere too much on the three canals down here.'

'Where can we talk?'

'If you want to talk about drugs is better you forget it.'

'I don't. I want to talk about a man. An Arab.'

'There's no Arab down these parts. I doubt if there are any in the whole city.'

'What about drugs from Iran and Afghanistan, and Pakistan?'

'When the drugs get here they have nobody but us.'

'There *is* an Arab in Amsterdam. He lives in a place on Nieuwe Leliestraat. His name's in the telephone book, Khalim Said. I want to find out about him.'

'What you want to find out?'

'Anything. Everything. And I want a room on the canals here where nobody knows who I am. And nobody cares.'

For long moments Jan Branders was silent. Looking over Rennie's shoulder at the people in the square. Finally he turned back to look at Rennie.

'Tell me what you're doing here.'

'Find out about Khalim Said for me and then maybe I'll tell you. But it's nothing to do with drugs, I promise you.'

'You swear that?'

'I swear it.'

Jan Branders smiled. 'I believe. You worry me too much coming out of the night like this.' He looked at his watch. 'I take you my place. Let's go. You keep with me all time.'

As they walked past the drug-pushers they shuffled out of the way, some of them saying a few words to Branders as they passed. He didn't respond to any of them. They came to a small, children's playground. A few yards further on Jan Branders turned round and made his way back down the street to a small alleyway on the right. A pretty coloured girl in a white leotard sat inside a lighted window and Jan Branders pushed a key into a door painted black. As it opened he pulled Rennie inside. There was a smell of incense or joss-sticks in the darkness and when Branders switched on the light there was a set of steep stairs facing them.

He followed up six flights of stairs past doors with double locks and no sounds from inside. Just once a door opened and a Chinese girl looked out; seeing Branders she closed the door again.

At the top of the stairs Jan turned keys in two separate locks, reached inside and switched on a light and waved Rennie inside.

The big room was nothing like he had expected. Plain white walls and white leather furniture. Even the carpet was white. It was straight out of *Vogue, House and Garden*, or some Swiss design magazine.

He turned to Branders. 'It's beautiful, Jan,' he smiled. 'You must be doing well.'

Branders was taking off his tatty rabbit-skin jacket, tossing it onto one of the big white leather armchairs. He walked over to a teak cabinet on the far wall.

'What you wish? Whisky, genever, English gin, vodka?'

Rennie smiled. 'Have you got a tomato juice?'

'Is only tinned.'

'That's fine.'

Branders bent down and opened the cupboard doors and took out two cans and a can-opener.

As Branders opened the cans and poured out the juice he said, 'You still with the same old mob, Johnny?'

'Yes.'

'That why you over here?'

'Yes.'

Branders handed him the drink and sat down facing Rennie.

'Tell me about your Arab.'

'He lives in a house on Nieuwe Leliestraat. Just beyond the small art gallery. He's rich. He's important, and I want to know all there is to know about him.'

'You got a photo of him?'

'No.'

'How much you pay for this?'

'Just for basic information and background . . . say two hundred guilders to start.'

'And why you want a room in the red-light district?'

'I want somewhere I can use that nobody knows about.'

'You mean police?'

'I mean everybody. Including my people.'

Branders nodded; he understood the need for such a place.

'I can let you have couple of rooms in Warmoesstraat. Is on edge of red-light area but not inside. Inside is not possible. You know Warmoesstraat? Is where you come over Old Bridge from the Damrak. There's a police station down the street.' He paused. 'You want to see it now?'

'If it's not too late for you.' Rennie paused. 'You look a bit tired.'

Branders finished the tomato juice and stood up, reaching for his jacket. 'Let's go.'

They crossed the two bridges and down the narrow alleyway, past the sex cinema and the peep-show and turned left into Warmoesstraat. He remembered it now he had seen it again. It was a narrow one-way street of shops, small hotels and the inevitable sex cinemas. There was a narrow pavement on one side of the street and a continuous line of parked cars on the opposite side. Jan Branders stopped a few houses beyond the bright yellow sign that said, 'Gay Cinema Adonis'. It was starting to rain.

As Branders stopped he searched his pockets for the key to the outer door and then realised that it wasn't locked. At the side of the door was a wooden plaque fastened to the wall and burned into its surface was a Chinese hieroglyph and the letters 'Jan B'. There was a smell of disinfectant as they walked up two flights of stairs and then Branders unlocked a door and waved Rennie into the darkness. When the light went on he saw a dingy room. Peeling paint on the brick walls, and plasterboard walls that marked off a small room with a bed. Along the far wall a stone sink. In the centre of the room was a cheap wooden table covered in worn oilcloth. The rest of the furnishings were cheap chairs and two roughly-made cupboards. Over the sink was a print of Princess Juliana. It reminded him suddenly of Mason's room in Paris.

Branders stood looking around the room as if it were as strange and new to him as it was to Rennie.

'Is OK for you, Johnny?'

Rennie turned and nodded. 'It's fine, Jan. How much?'

'Give me six hundred guilder and is yours for one year.'

'Can I pay you in sterling?'

'Anything except pesetas.'

'Are you sure that's enough?'

'I tell you if I need more sometime. You gonna live here?'

'No. I'll be here from time to time. I've got a place on the Prinsengracht.'

Branders gave him two keys. 'One for street. One for door here.'

'How can I contact you?'

'Go to my place. Ring bell three short and one long time. If I don't come down you go away.'

'Can you have lunch with me tomorrow?'

'What is lunch?'

'Midday.'

'OK. What time and where?'

'Twelve. You say where.'

'OK. Twelve at Restaurant Schiller in Rembrandtsplein. You know it?'

'I'll find it.'

'Is very busy. Is best you book for a table.'

'I'll bring the money for you.'

Branders shrugged his indifference, nodded, and walked out of the room. Rennie could hear his footsteps on the stairs and the sound of the street door closing. He looked around the room again. It was a depressing room, but it was just what he wanted. An escape hatch. If things went wrong he could abandon the apartment on Prinsengracht and hole up here until things quietened down. In an area like this people didn't care who you were or what you were doing. And being seen around by the locals could provide a useful alibi. It was somewhere he could meet the kind of people who'd look out of place on the Prinsengracht. He could keep the team's weapons here if it was necessary. In a dozen cities around the world Rennie had had similar hideaways and they had sometimes saved him from arrest, and at least twice had saved his life, because he was able to disappear from his usual territory. And because even SIS didn't know where he was. A few minutes later he walked through to the Damrak and waved down a taxi. It wasn't far to the Prinsengracht but suddenly he felt very tired.

Rennie slept until ten and shaved and dressed slowly. He found a bookshop and bought two street maps of Amsterdam, a paperback guide in English and a Berlitz phrase book.

The rain of the previous evening had cleared and the sky was blue. He walked over the Old Bridge and down War-moesstraat past the rooms. It all looked slightly more civil-ised in daylight. Locals shopping and bicycles leaning against walls. A car or two threaded its way cautiously down the street. At the far end workmen were fitting a sign over an empty shop. He had forgotten to book the table at the restaurant and took a taxi to Rembrandtsplein. There was one vacant table. He ordered a coffee and told the waitress that he was waiting for a friend.

Branders came a quarter of an hour early and they ordered the soup of the day and fish. Branders was dressed in jeans and a check shirt and hadn't shaved, but he seemed at home in the restaurant. The waitress had chatted to him in Dutch as if they knew one another well.

When they got to the fish Branders said quietly, 'Your Arab. Age is early forties. Like you say he is very rich. All his business is big contracts. Gover'ment contracts. Engin-eering. Construction. Hospitals, hotels, cars, tractors. He gets piece of action from both sides. All legal and in writing.

'His wife is Italian girl from Milan. Twenty-seven years old. Very, very pretty. Name Gabriella. Two childs. Boy seven, girl four or five. Not sure. He has many friends but not many people at their house. Two servants. One Dutch woman for wife and childs. An Indian for house and drive car. A Filipino cook comes in every day. Seven days a week.

'No drugs. No girls. No boys. Genuine Islam. Makes Haj to Mecca every year. He's a straight guy.'

'Any contact with terrorists?'

Branders shrugged. 'Would take time to find that out. He don't look like that sort of guy.' He shrugged again. 'But with Arabs who can tell?' He pronounced Arabs the American way and he went on: 'Arabs most of the time quiet people like my people, but sometimes they go crazy. You seen my people when they explode.'

Rennie said casually, 'Have you heard any rumours of Arab terrorists moving into this area?'

'Are you after terrorists, Johnny?'

For a moment Rennie hesitated. Then he nodded. 'There's a group of Arabs holding one of our men. I want to get him back.'

'You mean they kidnapped him?'

'Yes.'

'If they did that they'll do a deal, Johnny. They'll want money to fund their operations.'

'They don't want money, Jan. They've already said what they want.'

'What is it?'

'I can't tell you, but we don't want to go along with it. I've got to get our guy back as soon as possible.'

'You got people to help you?'

'They'll come over when I want them.'

'How much you pay for some help?'

'Tell me what you want.'

Branders looked intently at Rennie's face for several moments and then looked down at his coffee as he stirred it slowly. Without looking up he said, 'You think I forget you saved my life, yes?'

'That was a long time ago, Jan. Forget it.'

'I never forget, my friend. Is maybe other mens would have got me out but they would want in return. Money, drugs – they want something. And I would have paid. Being glad to pay. You ask me nothing. In fac' you give me hundert pounds sterling to give me a start.' He smiled. 'With your money I buy drugs. I make nice profit. Soon I make big, big money. I got money in banks all over the world. Dollars, yen, D-marks, Swiss francs, gold and diamonds.' Branders smiled. 'Same as you do. In Amsterdam is more than twenty people work for me now.'

He nodded. 'I pay you any way you like. Cash, girls, drugs or . . . I help you any way you want. I've not forgot what you did for me. They would have killed you too.'

Rennie smiled. 'Forget it, Jan. Nobody's ever gonna kill me.'

Branders grinned. 'You still know all those tricks?'

'And more. I never stop learning.'

'So what you want me to do next?'

'Can you have the Arab watched. I want a pattern of his day. Where he goes. What the family does. What kind of protection does he have at the house?'

'You going in after him?'

'Not if there's some other way.'

'He don't look like terrorist to me.'

'He isn't. But he's the go-between.'

'OK. Give me your address in Prinsengracht.' When he saw Rennie's face he laughed softly. 'I not come myself, I send somebody better.'

Rennie smiled. 'How long do you need?'

'One day. Maybe two to make sure. If you are in the rooms in Warmoesstraat you put a white chalk cross on the wooden sign by the door. When you leave you wipe off.'

Rennie paid the bill and as they walked past the bar to the outer door Branders said, 'How your wife?'

'We're divorced, Jan. About a year ago.'

Branders nodded without comment. 'If you want girl you tell me. No problem.'

'Thanks.'

Branders looked across the square and a car parked by the public telephone boxes moved out and came forward as Branders stepped into the road. The rear door opened and Branders nodded to Rennie as he got inside.

A note had been pushed under the door at the flat on Prinsengracht. It was from Lambert, the SIS man based at the Amsterdam consulate at Johannes Vermeerstraat. Lambert wanted him to phone as soon as possible.

Rennie dialled the number and the telephonist put him through to Lambert. Lambert suggested a meeting by the bank in the Central Station in half an hour.

Rennie bought a *Daily Mail* at the papershop in the station and walked along the passage to the bank. He stood looking at the headlines. The usual strikes, a bomb attack on an Israeli settlement on the West Bank and a pop-star fined £50 for possession of a gram of marijuana. A bored sermon from the magistrate and the usual claim by the pop-star to reporters outside the court that marijuana was less harmful than gin or cigarettes. And then Lambert arrived.

'Hi, Johnny.'

'Hi. What's the panic?'

'No panic, but I had a mysterious message a couple of days ago from Paynter. Said I was to find you a lead to this Arab named Khalim Said. Preferably a woman. Said it was urgent so I've been scouting around.'

'What have you got?'

'Her name's Adele Palmer. Twenty-seven or eight. Divorced. British subject. Owns a gallery not far from your place. Attractive, intelligent, easy-going and she's been a friend of the Said family for a year or so.'

'What kind of tale can I give her?'

'Whatever your cover is. I don't want to know. Paynter told me to ask you no questions. There's no problem with her, her father was in SOE and then in SIS. He retired about five years ago. Heart trouble of some sort. I've used her from time to time to get me routine information. We both pretend it's so that HM Consul can invite the right people to his dinner parties. Or at least know what they've been up to if he *has* to ask them for some reason or other. And we help her in various ways.

'If you want, I can contact her and tell her that you'd like to get alongside Khalim Said and that we'd like her to fix it. She'll want to be assured that it's all in a good cause and that Said isn't being involved in anything.'

Rennie half-smiled. 'She sounds OK to me. Will you phone me when you've arranged for me to meet her?'

'Sure. Is it urgent?'

'Yes.'

'I don't want to know what you're up to but I hope it isn't

going to have repercussions on us or the embassy in The Hague.'

'It shouldn't. If it looks like blowing up I'll warn you, if there's time.'

'It's bloody difficult operating out of the consulate. You'd think I was KGB rather than SIS.'

Rennie shrugged. 'You should be used to that by now. Anyway, thanks for the contact. I'll keep away from you as much as I can.'

'If you're desperate you can use my direct line to London. It's got scrambler facilities.'

'Thanks.'

Lambert hesitated for a moment as if he was embarrassed and then said, 'Cheers,' and walked back towards the main entrance of the station.

Rennie walked to the entrance and stood in the shadow of one of the pillars as he watched Lambert get into a taxi.

If you were part of SIS's 'dirty-tricks' set-up you didn't trust anyone. Not even those who were supposed to be on your side. Trust anyone and you could easily end up face-down in some canal or with a knife in your back in some alleyway. There was a scar that ran from his shoulder to his belly that was a constant reminder of what could happen if you trusted when you shouldn't. But Johnny Rennie had never been scared since he was a boy. His natural characteristics and his training made fear seem a waste of time. He was a hunter not the hunted. There were no niceties or Queensberry Rules in his life. Sitting ducks were there to be shot. It wasn't competitive. Once the target was in your sights you pulled the trigger, or tightened the noose, whatever the situation called for. You didn't get into fights because you were trained to kill not fight. Fighting was for amateurs.

He walked down the Damrak and turned off to the sleazy room in Warmoesstraat. He bought food and a few pieces of crockery and cutlery, a frying pan and two saucepans and took them back to the room.

There was one small window and in the late afternoon sun the room looked less forbidding. He spent an hour cleaning it up and then walked back to his apartment.

The phone was ringing as he let himself in. It was Lambert. He'd talked to the woman and there was no problem. She could be contacted anytime he wanted. Lambert gave him her gallery and private numbers and the address of the gallery. She lived over the premises.

Chapter 10

THE GALLERY was on a corner, and as Rennie walked in, a woman sitting at a small teak desk smiled as she looked him over.

'I'm guessing that you're English. Please look around. The prices are on the little white stars on the frames.'

'Are you Adele Palmer?'

'Yes.'

'I'm John Rennie.'

'Please feel free to look around, Mr Rennie.'

'Mr Lambert at the consulate said he'd mentioned my name to you.'

'Of course. How silly of me. It didn't register.' She stood up and walked over to him. 'Peter Lambert said you wanted an introduction to a friend of mine.'

'I'd be much obliged if you could do that.'

The brown eyes looked him over and then she said, 'Khalim Said is a special friend of mine. His family too. I don't want to pry but I take it that your motives for meeting him are – what shall I say? – above-board. Not to his detriment.'

Rennie's face was impassive as he said, 'You don't need to worry, Ms Palmer.'

'How would you like to do this?'

'As casually as you can. Do you see them often?'

'Most days I pop in for an hour or so in the evening.'

'Perhaps I could take you to dinner tonight or tomorrow. I could be a friend of yours from England and we drop in to see them after we have eaten.'

'Let me phone them and see if it's convenient.'

She spoke in Italian and he guessed she was speaking to

the Arab's wife. There was a lot of girlish laughter and then she put her hand over the phone.

'Gabriella says why don't we eat with them tonight.'

'Fine. What time shall I call for you?'

'About eight OK?'

'Of course.'

She spoke again on the telephone and then hung up. She smiled. 'See you at eight. It's in walking distance from here. About ten minutes.

'I'll call for you at a quarter to.'

'OK. Ring the bell on the side door. My name's on the card.'

'Thanks for your help.'

'Not at all.'

Rennie wore his one and only good suit and took a taxi because of the flowers. Adele Palmer was obviously surprised and pleased and insisted on putting them into a vase before they left.

Her living room was feminine and cosy and on the wall there was a drawing in *sanguine* of a naked girl. An Annigoni. The photographs clustered on an antique table were all of females and Rennie was aware of the oblique but obvious message. It made things easier.

It was still sunny, and the narrow Amsterdam streets looked at their best. Rennie was seldom aware of his surroundings apart from their effect on whatever he was doing, but he found the medieval houses and streets strangely appealing. Amsterdam was a city that represented many things that he admired. There was nothing contrived or phoney about its beauty or its people. The city and its inhabitants seem to have moved through the centuries calmly, without being caught up in the race for skyscrapers and neon lights.

A servant answered the door and Gabriella Said was waiting for them at the top of the stairs. She looked younger than he had expected and she was strikingly beautiful. He had expected a typically extrovert Italian girl but she was both shy and gentle, her large brown eyes constantly on her husband's face. And she admired, smiling, the bunch of roses that Rennie had brought for her before she led them into the large living room.

Khalim Said was tall and not quite handsome, but his face was alive and his black eyes alert. He smiled easily with an almost boyish laugh. His skin was no darker than would come from a season's tan at St Tropez and the slightly aquiline nose could make a casual observer assume that he was a Jew. There was black hair on the backs of his hands but his long tapering fingers were almost white with carefully manicured nails. The movements of his hands and arms were surprisingly graceful for a man. Each gesture, even the most ordinary, seemed to be choreographed and controlled. But it was obviously instinctive and natural and not contrived. His English was fluent and without any foreign accent, but he interposed an Arabic word from time to time when he was speaking to his wife.

The music coming from the concealed speakers was a slow, languorous guitar, a mixture of Spain and North Africa. Long, haunting strands of single notes without chords, reminiscent of de Falla and 'Nights in the Gardens of Spain'.

After the meal they sat in the tiled living room, Said and his wife together on a brocade settee, her long slim fingers just touching his brown hand as they all chatted together. Eventually Said looked at Rennie, smiling as he said, 'I know it's terribly bad manners to ask, Mr Rennie, but I'm curious. What do you do?'

Rennie smiled back. 'Guess.'

Said looked intently at Rennie's face before he spoke. Then he said, slowly and thoughtfully, 'If I didn't know already that you are a civilian I would have said that you were a soldier.'

Rennie laughed. 'Why that?'

'You look four-square on the world from those brown eyes of yours. And there is something about your mouth that says you are used to giving orders and having them obeyed. I see no doubts in your face. It's an honest face but a cautious face.' Said laughed. 'And now tell me that you are a poet who writes of love, and stars in the evening sky.'

Rennie shook his head, still smiling. 'Like most men I served in the army a long time ago but I'm not a professional soldier. I work for a firm of solicitors in London.'

'I'm surprised. Very surprised. Do you defend people or prosecute them?'

'Neither. I'm an investigator.'

'How interesting. Tell me. Why do solicitors need investigators?'

'Most solicitors use free-lance investigators. The firm that I work for is quite large. So it's more economical to employ someone full-time.'

'And what do you investigate?'

Rennie shrugged. 'Documents, relationships, suspected fraud, missing persons, stolen valuables.' He paused. 'Anything and everything.'

'It must be very satisfactory to help the innocent. But what if you suspect your company's client is guilty?'

Rennie laughed. 'My company's clients are never guilty. Anyway, that's for a court to decide and by the time it gets to court my work is almost always over.'

'What are you looking for in Amsterdam, may I ask?'

'I'm afraid I can't say very much. It's a missing person – a girl.'

'How sad that a daughter should leave her home and family.' Said shrugged. 'But we live in a time of turmoil. As if the whole world is bubbling like a cauldron on a fire.'

'Can I ask you something, Mr Said?'

'Khalim, please. Of course.'

'Where did you learn such perfect English?'

Said laughed, his strong teeth exposed for a moment, and Rennie realised then how attractive he must be to women. It wouldn't have been all that difficult for him to ease Fleur Mason into bed.

'I went to university in England and business school in the USA. My American friends say it's a genuine Oxford accent and my English friends say it's obviously Bostonian.' He paused. 'It's a language I love. It's like Arabic in a way. Gentle and descriptive. Made for poets and story-tellers.'

Adele interrupted. 'Tell us an Arabic story, Khalim.

Please.'

Said laughed. 'You westerners are terrible. You've been deceived by all those stories of Scheherazade. Magic carpets and belly-dancers. We're not like that any more. We never were, for that matter.' He looked at Rennie and then at Adele. 'Tell me – what is an Arab? How do you define it?'

Adele said briskly, 'Someone who believes in Mohammed. A Moslem – or is it a Muslim?'

Said shook his head. 'There are Christian Arabs and Jewish Arabs.' He smiled and looked at Rennie. 'Your definition, Mr Rennie?'

'People who live in an Arab country.'

Said was quiet for a moment. 'Would you say Israel was an Arab country . . . I was born there.'

Rennie said quietly, 'I imagine that you see it still as an Arab country.'

'I do. And it is of course. My family have been there for at least three hundred years. Until the British gave our land and our homes to the Jews to salve their consciences about the gas-chambers.'

'But the Arabs could have stayed.'

'So why am I here? Why aren't I in Jerusalem in the home where I was born? Why are my mother and father dead, and my sister living in Detroit? Tell me.'

Adele said softly, 'Don't get upset, Khalim. Let's forget it. Let's talk about art or music. Anything but that.'

Said's wife said something to him softly, in Arabic, but he shook his head.

'It has to be said. It was done. It is part of history.' He took a deep breath. 'My father was a judge – a *Khadi*. We had a big house and several hundred acres of orange and lemon groves. Bought and paid for by my grandfather and his father. We had Jews in Palestine long before the Mandate and long before the UN gave our land to the Jews. But there were at least two Palestinians for every Jew. The Jews were a minority in an Arab land.

'In 1948 Palestine was partitioned and part became Israel. No Palestinian was asked if he agreed. It was just done. Palestine was not just colonised. Six hundred thousand Palestinians were evicted from their homes. There was no compensation. We were evicted and looted. By force. Against our will and against all natural justice. But the figures are just figures. What they represent was countless personal tragedies. The burning of villages, bull-dozing homes and property, killings of innocent people, massacres of whole communities. Women and girls raped. Respected public figures deliberately humiliated.

'We moved from the official judge's house in Tel Aviv to the family home in Jerusalem. My father counselled calmness and restraint. Two years later he was shot in the gardens of our home. So was my mother. My sister was already in Damascus. In one day they wiped out my family's history. With guns and hatred.'

Said brushed a tear from his eye and the others sat in silence. There was nothing to say. If there was, they didn't know what it was.

It was Adele who broke the silence. 'Let me play you something, Khalim, and then we'll go,' she said quietly.

Khalim nodded and sighed as he stood up and followed her through the wide archway.

Adele pushed the silk scarf back over her shoulder and sat down at the piano. She played a few random quiet chords and then she sang in a childish voice, thin, quavering but sweet. And Khalim smiled at last as he recognised the words of the Brahms lullaby – '*Guten Abend, Gute Nacht, von Rosen bedacht . . .*'

It was as nearly right for their mood as anything could have been.

They were all conscious of the tension but Adele chattered quietly with Gabriella and kissed Khalim gently as they said their goodbyes.

As they walked back together towards the gallery they were silent for most of the time and then Adele said, 'Arabs must hate us Europeans.'

'There's a lot of Europeans hate the Arabs. Their record isn't all that good.'

'In what way?'

'Killings. The Munich Olympics. The PLO. Bombing and shelling civilians. The Arab countries all put their own interests first. There could have been a Palestinian state on the West Bank years ago. And what have any of the Arab States done for their people? Without oil they'd be back in the deserts. And the oil won't last for ever.'

'But what right had anybody to give other people's land and houses to the Israelis?'

'None. But it wasn't the British who gave it away, it was the UN.'

'But they didn't have any right to do that either.'

'Too true. But it's done, and now all the Palestinians are trying to do is put the clock back. And they won't be able to do it. Nobody can. History has moved on. They should do a deal and settle somewhere and make that a new Palestine.'

'But you can't expect them just to forget what's been done to them.'

'They have to learn to forget. It's the only way. All over the world nations have done terrible things to other nations. The Danes and the Normans and Romans to Britain. Britain to the Irish. Someday you have to cry halt to the bitterness or the killing goes on for centuries until it has nothing to do with the original crimes. The world's got tired of the Palestinians. They're just killing for the sake of it. Murdering just to keep themselves in the news. But there's people all over the world doing just the same. Kampuchea, El Salvador, Nicaragua, all over Africa, and the Arabs aren't news any more.'

'But a man like Khalim would understand all that. And he obviously still cares.'

'D'you want a drink before you turn in? It might take your mind off tonight.'

'Where can we go at this time of night?'

'I'll take you for a drink at The Pulitzer and then walk you home.'

'Fine,' she paused. 'Did you like Khalim?'

Rennie smiled. 'I liked them both and they obviously count you as one of the family.'

Then they were at the hotel. From the corner of his eye Rennie could see a man leaning casually against the wall by the door of his own flat.

As Rennie walked back towards his flat he tried to reconstruct the layout of the Said apartment. But his mind was hindered by the thought of the man lounging by his own front door. He stopped at the corner that led the side street into the Prinsengracht. The man was still there. He could see the glow from his cigarette in the darkness.

As he walked across the bridge the man came towards him and Rennie saw the glowing arc as the man flicked his cigarette over the rails alongside the canal. The man stood squarely in front of him, blocking his path, and as Rennie raised his arm to push him aside the man said gruffly, '*Ik kom van Jan Branders.*' He paused and said slowly, 'You come . . . with . . . me . . . to . . . Jan . . . now . . . he waits . . . for you.'

'Where is Jan?'

The man turned and pointed towards the church and said, 'Kom.'

Without waiting to see if Rennie followed him the man turned and walked along the street towards the church. There was nobody outside the church and the man walked on ahead. At Noorder Markt he stopped and Rennie saw the headlights of a car flash briefly in the side street.

As he approached he saw Jan Branders at the wheel of the black Mercedes. Jan leaned across and opened the passenger door, and Rennie got in.

Branders smiled. 'You tekking out ladies already, my friend?'

Rennie didn't respond. 'What is it, Jan?'

Branders looked away, staring through the windscreen towards the canal.

'I got problems and you got problems.'

'What's my problem?'

Jan laughed softly, 'Your problem is I got problem.'

'I'm tired, Jan. Let's get on with it.'

Branders reached inside his jacket, took out an envelope and handed it to Rennie. 'Is report on what Said family do . . . like you asked. Is from inside. All correct.'

'Thanks. Is that the problem?'

'No. No, my friend. Is difficult to tell you of problem.'

'Why?'

'I think I know who got your man.'

'Where is he?' Rennie said quickly.

'Slow, slow. I said *who* got him not where he is.'

'So who's got him?'

'Is one Arab is boss but like you they come to Surinamese for help.'

'Tell me more.'

'Surinamese is my countrymen, old friend. You want for me to get them in jail?'

Rennie sighed. 'Just tell me where he is and leave it to me. There's no question of jail.'

Branders shook his head. 'I told you I don't know where he is. All I know is one Arab and four, five Surinamese got a white man as prisoner.'

'How did you find this out?'

'I sent word out. It came back to me.'

'D'you think it's true?'

Jan Branders laughed softly, 'Nobody tell lie to me, Johnny. Is better dead they do that.'

'Is he in Amsterdam?'

'No.'

'In Holland?'

'Yes.'

'What else do you know?'

'I know they have him on a boat. And that's all I know.'

'Can you find out more?'

'I don't think so. Maybe money would work but I don't think so. If my man say more they kill him for sure.'

'So why did he tell you this much?'

'He owe me plenty from way back. I make him talk . He scared of me now but much more he is scared of the Arab and the others.'

'How does he know what he knows?'

'The Surinam men are addicts. Heroin and opium. My man is their supplier.'

'Can I talk with your man?'

'No. Definitely no. Never.' Branders shook his head vehemently.

Rennie took a deep breath. 'Well . . . thank you, Jan, for what you've told me. And for the report. If you hear any more that you feel you can tell me I'd be very grateful for your help.'

Jan Branders turned his head quickly to look at Rennie. 'You think I know more than I tell you, don't you?'

'Yes.'

Branders looked away and sat silent for several moments.

'If I hear more I contact you. If you get in trouble – use my name.'

Rennie patted Branders's hand on the steering-wheel and let himself out of the car.

Chapter 11

THE PHONE rang several times before Rennie turned in his bed and reached out to lift the phone.

'Rennie.'

'I'm booked in at the Amstel, Johnny. How about you come over?'

It was Paynter and Rennie said, 'I'll be about an hour. You booked in your name?'

'Of course.'

'See you later.' And Rennie hung up.

The taxi pulled up at the foot of the steps of the Amstel Hotel and a doorman opened the door for Rennie and helped him out.

Rennie found it typical of Paynter to have booked in at the Amstel. It was a cross between the Connaught and the Ritz. Quiet, impressive, old-fashioned, and luxurious by any standards.

The hall-porter phoned Paynter's room and Paynter asked for him to go up.

'Room 329, sir. The lift's on the left. Thank you, sir.'

Paynter opened the door before he knocked and pointed to the table in the window.

'I've got coffee for us both. Sit yourself down.'

As Rennie stirred his coffee Paynter said, 'You've only had a few days. How are things going?'

'I've met Khalim Said and his wife. And I can confirm that Mason is being held in Holland. I don't know where but he's on a boat. There's an Arab in charge and the others are Surinamese.'

'You've not been wasting your time, have you? How did you get on to Mason?'

'An old contact. A Surinamese.'

'Is this the chap you raised hell about way back when you wanted to get him out?'

'That's the one.'

'Well, my news is not so startling but it's useful. We sent two ordnance and electronics chaps out to Damascus and they were taken down to a place called Rayak in the Beka'a valley, just over the Syrian border in Lebanon.

'We don't really know who we're dealing with but it's a mixed bag of Syrians and Iranians. They've got this RPV, a remote piloted vehicle, that's got some fault in its electronics and also they don't know how to operate it. They've got their own electronics guy watching our chaps like a hawk, but he's got no experience on anything as sophisticated as this.

'They've offered our chaps money, girls, the lot. All on the side. Swiss bank accounts and all the trimmings and we've told them to look cooperative within reason.

'But there's two snags. The first is that our communication with our two fellows is pretty tenuous and secondly we suspect that we can't trust either the Syrians or the Iranians to keep to the bargain.'

'Why didn't the Arabs get the Russians to fix the equipment?'

Paynter shrugged. 'Probably don't want the Russians to know they've got it.'

'How important is it to the Arabs? The equipment.'

'It's very important. It could help them give the Israeli ground forces a real beating.'

'What does it do?'

'You know me, Johnny. Can hardly fix a fuse. But from what they tell me they can shuffle these things around just on a lorry. It's a pilotless plane. They launch the bloody thing on a battle front and it sends back high-resolution TV pictures covering sixteen square miles. Shows everything on the ground. You can guide it where you want and bring it back. The Israeli ground forces have always relied on surprise and they'd be sitting ducks for any guerrillas if they had this little gadget.'

'And if our guys fix this, will they release Mason, d'you think?'

'Well, one of the technicians we sent is an Arab-speaker and we think he's trying to hint that they're just using us. Unfortunately the Arabs are deliberately using a dialect where he can only get a rough idea of what they're saying to one another. I wouldn't trust the bastards myself.'

'So we have to operate here like they aren't going to deliver.'

'Looks a bit like it. Maybe I'll know more in the next few days. But have a contingency plan in mind for a last resort.'

'And Said is definitely involved?'

'Oh sure. All the messages from our two chaps come back through him. He contacts us daily. I generally speak to him myself. Smooth, charming and amiable. Tries to give the impression that it's all something he'd rather have no hand in. Above this sort of caper.' Paynter laughed. 'Doesn't stop him from putting on all the pressure he can. Was terribly hurt and indignant when I asked him if his friends in the Lebanon were to be trusted to keep their part of the bargain.'

'I'd guess he genuinely doesn't like it all that much. He's the wrong type for this kind of business.'

'Maybe. But the fact is he does it. And it's facts that count in my book.' He reached over to his open case on the bed. 'Got some mail for you.' As he handed over a manilla envelope he said, 'Anything else you want while I'm over here?'

'Nothing at the moment.'

He stood up and Rennie took the hint. They shook hands and Paynter escorted him to the door.

Chapter 12

HE SAW the crowd of young people and the flashing light on the police van as he came over the canal bridge. He could hear the shouting and cursing in half a dozen languages as he approached the crowd. Then he realised who they were. They were young squatters from the basements of the two empty houses opposite his room, and the police were evicting them. Suddenly the crowd broke away, running down the street towards the lights at the far end. All except a girl who sat on the cobbles clutching a small bundle, her head bowed over her drawn-up knees.

A policeman said something to her and she looked up slowly, her face deathly pale in the moonlight. And slowly and clearly she said, in English, 'Why don't you fuck off, you bastards.'

As the policeman reached for her thin arm Rennie bent down towards the girl and said, 'What's the matter?'

'Tell those pigs to leave me alone.'

Rennie straightened up and looked at the policeman. Shaking his head, as he said, 'Can I help? What's the problem? I'm afraid I can't speak Dutch.' He paused. 'Has she committed an offence?'

The policeman shrugged. 'We have orders from the court to evict the squatters. We can't let her go back in the house again.'

'Let me talk to her. I'll see that she doesn't go back in.'

'Are you a tourist, mijnheer?'

Rennie nodded towards the house. 'I live here, officer. I've got rooms in that house.'

The policeman shouted in Dutch to one of the other policemen who said something brief in reply. He turned back to Rennie. 'If she is here in one hour she will be taken into custody.' He frowned and said, 'She is not safe in these streets at this hour.'

'I'll look after her.'

'OK. But you must warn her or she will be taken as a vagrant.'

When the police van had reversed out of the street Rennie looked down at the girl. Her head was resting on her knees, one hand on the small cheap plastic hold-all beside her on the cobbles.

He crouched down beside her and said, 'Are you English?'

She shook her head.

'American?'

The girl lifted her face slowly and looked at Rennie.

'Just leave me alone.'

'You heard what he said, they'll pick you up if you stay here.'

She shrugged her thin shoulders. 'So what.'

'Have you eaten?' It was the only thing he could think of to say.

She just looked away towards the lights at the far end of the street and said nothing. Rennie put his hand gently on her bony shoulder.

'I live in the house there. Come and have a coffee and a sandwich.'

He stood up slowly, taking her hand. For a moment she hesitated and then she stood up unsteadily, her eyes closed. Rennie put his arm round her and walked her to the door of the house.

When he switched on the light in his room he saw how ill she looked. The white face, the brown patches under her eyes and the almost bloodless lips. Now that she was inside the room she seemed to have lost her defiance. She sat obediently when he pointed to the chair, and when he came back with a cheese sandwich, a cold sausage and mugs of coffee she sat with him at the rickety table and ate slowly without talking or looking at him.

'Where do you live?'

She shook her head.

'What's that mean?'

'I don't live anywhere. I just bum around.'

'Where are you from?'

'Are you English?' As the girl looked at him he realised that she was on some drug. Her pupils were dilated and her breathing was shallow.

'Yes.'

She shrugged. 'I nearly went to London instead of this place. London sounds grim.'

'Look, girl, it's nearly 3 a.m. There's a bed in the next room. I'll fix myself up out here. Get some sleep and then you can decide what you want to do.'

'What's your name?'

'Johnny.'

'OK. But I got bad news for you, Johnny. I don't screw just for a bed.'

The girl saw the aggression in Rennie's eyes as he said, 'There's a key in the bedroom door, honey. It works just as well from the inside.' He stood up, collecting the dirty crockery from the table. As she picked up her plastic hold-all she half-smiled, then walked to the bedroom.

He fried four eggs and grilled half a dozen narrow strips of lean bacon. And when he had poured the coffee into the mugs he knocked on the bedroom door.

'Time to eat, girl. It's getting cold.'

Rennie didn't wait for an answer, he expected her to do as she was told.

Five minutes later she joined him at the table. And as she ate he covertly looked at her. Her long lank hair looked as if it hadn't been washed in weeks and her skin was pallid, her hands shaking as she held the knife and fork. But he saw that she must have been very pretty before she let herself go. She ate slowly and reluctantly as if she found the food distasteful. She didn't look at him as she ate and when she had finished she put her bony hands around the warm mug as if to warm them before she lifted the mug to her mouth.

'What's your name, girl?'

'Joanna. Joanna de Vries.'

'You speak very good English.'

For the first time she looked at his face. 'I'm not Dutch. I'm American. My grandparents were Dutch.'

'How old are you?'

'Twenty.'

'Are you on holiday here?'

'No. I live here.'

'What do you do?'

'I don't understand?'

'What's your job?'

She shook her head. 'I don't have a work permit.'

'How do you get by? For food and things.'

She shrugged. 'I share with other squatters. I've got some savings. Not much. But I manage.'

'You like it here?'

'Not really.'

'So why stay?'

'I've nowhere else to go.'

'What about your home back in the States?'

'They don't want me.' She sighed and hesitated. 'My father. He threw me out.'

Rennie collected up the plates and cutlery and walked over to the sink. As he washed them in the bowl he thought about the girl. She looked ill, and he wondered if she was a confirmed addict. But she would fit in well with his cover of looking for a missing girl. As he dried his hands he turned and looked at her. She was still sitting at the table, her head bowed, her hands around the mug.

'What were you planning to do today?'

She shrugged. 'I don't know. I'll go looking for the squatters. They'll have found some place by now.'

'Are they friends of yours?'

'No. They're just squatters.'

He sat down at the table facing her and said softly, 'Are you on drugs, Joanna?'

'Only hash. I was never much into anything else. Anyway I can't afford the real stuff any more.'

'I shan't be using my rooms for a couple of days. Would you like to stay here and rest up for a bit?'

'I can't pay. There's not enough for that.'

'You don't have to pay. There's food and a bed. Just help yourself.'

'Why? Why are you helping me?'

Rennie shrugged. 'No particular reason. But you obviously need some help.'

'I'm no good in bed, if that's what you want. They all say that.'

For long moments Rennie looked at the girl's face. And for the first time he noticed the clear blue of her eyes. The same blue as his daughter's eyes. He smiled and said, 'Just clear up the place a bit for me. That's all. And you don't have to do even that unless you want to.'

He stood up and took the two spare keys that he'd had made from the ring and put them on the table. 'The big one's for the street door. I'm not sure when I'll be back. Two, maybe three days. If you go, leave the keys on the table.'

'What's your name?'

'John. John Rennie.'

As he opened the door he turned and looked at her. 'Take care of yourself. See you.'

Her eyes were looking at the mug in her hands and she didn't look at him as he left.

Adele Palmer had invited him to the opening of a new artist's show at the gallery and the whole Said family was there. Khalim, Gabriella, their son Jamal and the little girl, Nadia.

The pictures were modern, not the kind of work that Rennie could admire or even understand but there were a dozen red 'sold' stars already on the frames. Said had bought two and was enthusiastic about them, chatting knowledgeably to the girl artist. The pictures he had bought were presents for a member of the Saudi royal family and Said was sure that they would certainly lead to other purchases.

Rennie had invited them all to drinks that night but the children's nurse had her day off and they invited him and

Adele back to their apartment instead.

They all walked back together to the Saids' apartment, the Saids holding hands and walking ahead. Adele Palmer said quietly, 'Are you married, Johnny?'

'Divorced.'

'Any children?'

'Two daughters.'

'How old are they?'

'Round about the same age as Khalim's kids.'

'Do you see them at all?'

'Most weekends.'

'Do you miss then when you're away?'

It was several seconds before Rennie replied. 'I never spend time regretting things that can't be changed. Only fools do that.'

Adele Palmer smiled. 'Fools and women.'

Rennie nodded. 'Yes. And women. It's their nature. Too much time to think and dwell on things.'

He was quite unconscious of the jibe at his character.

After they had eaten they stayed talking at the table. About the show at the gallery. Music. Films and books. It was Adele who had brought up the subject of Arabic script and Said's eyes had lit up as he talked.

'For us Arabs the word is everything. And that beautiful script is part of the word. Just twelve basic shapes and a few dots and there is art as well as communication. That's what we have from the Qur'ān. The Qur'ān is the word. It rules all good Muslims' lives. It's our rock.' He looked at Rennie, smiling. 'Do words mean a lot to you, Johnny?'

'Not like they do to you.'

'But think of the influence that English words have had on the whole world.'

'Like what?'

'Like Dickens who made us all aware of the plight of the poor. *Uncle Tom's Cabin* and the slaves. Your beautiful translation of the Scriptures. You don't have to be a Christian to appreciate the wisdom of the Bible. Think of the Sermon on the Mount. Nobody has ever said in so few words, and more beautifully, how a man should live.'

Rennie smiled. 'Do you really believe that the meek will

inherit the earth?'

Adele Palmer laughed softly. 'He's got you there, Khalim.'

Said turned quickly towards her. 'No. No. You cannot take just one precept and criticise it.' He looked back at Rennie. 'Take the big conflicts of the world today. Communism and Christianity. If you read the words with understanding there is almost no difference between them. They would both work – but nobody tries to make them work. The Russians are not communists and the West are not Christians. If it were not for people either belief would work.'

'And what about the Jews and the Arabs. The Talmud and the Qur'ān?'

Gabriella held up her hand. 'No. Please no more. It's all been said so many times. But nobody listens.'

Said smiled. 'Just one more sentence, my love. The last word privilege of a host.'

She shrugged and smiled, reaching out for his hand, holding it as he turned back to look at Rennie.

'The problem with us, the Jews and the Arabs, is not our differences. The problem *is* . . . that we are too alike. We understand each other too well. We are like children of the same parents, quarrelling like siblings. We are from the same forebears, we lived in the same lands, our language is almost the same. Remember what I said about the word. There is not much difference between saying "shalom" and saying "salaam alyekum".'

'So why the fighting, the assassinations, the bombings of innocent people?'

'You want to remember something. The Qur'ān is the Old Testament, not the New. The Jews spread all over the world. The Arabs stayed in their lands. Our lands were taken from us by outsiders and given to the Jews. What we fight for now is justice. The West has pushed us back to the old laws. An eye for an eye. A tooth for a tooth.'

'But there could be a State of Palestine on the West Bank right now.'

Said shook his head disparagingly. 'Just imagine that after the war the United Nations had said that there are a lot of Jews in Bradford so we give them Yorkshire and Lancashire as a Jewish state. People's land and houses are taken and they are driven out of where they lived for decades. Then later, to keep others quiet the Jews say, OK. Stop being a nuisance. We give you a small piece back. A piece we were never given originally but we took by force. A piece of Derbyshire. We say we give you Derbyshire and we keep the rest. Would the English not fight back? Tell me, honestly.'

Rennie shook his head. 'There's a point beyond which you don't go. A line you don't cross.'

'What point, Johnny? What line?'

'Killing innocent women and children. Assassinating people just to get a headline in some crummy newspaper.'

'Is that how you see the Arabs?'

'No. But when the Palestinians said they would kill every Israeli – man, woman and child – they went back into the dark ages and the world isn't willing to go back with them into that dark night.'

'So what should we do?'

'Talk. Negotiate.'

'We tried that right at the start. Nobody listened.'

'They'll listen now. It's the PLO who won't listen.'

Said shook his head, trying to smile. 'We shan't solve the problem tonight, Johnny. It's a mad world we've all made and . . .'He paused. '. . . I saw a musical in London years ago called *Stop the World I Want to Get Off.* I think I would like that. To stop the world for a week so that we can all think again about what we want.'

'What do *you* want, Khalim?' Rennie said quietly.

Said leaned back in his chair, closing his eyes, thinking. Then he opened his eyes and leaned forward, looking at Rennie.

'I would like it to be evening. The sun just going down. To walk in a garden with Gabriella and our two children. And say to them, "Pick an orange off one of the trees as I did when I was a child. As my father did. And his father. And all the way back. In this same garden where I belong and you belong." ' Said looked at Rennie and sighed. 'Is that asking too much? Or should the garden stay as it is

94

now, occupied by an Israeli anti-riot squad. I love that place, Johnny. It's where I belong.' Said turned suddenly to Adele Palmer. 'Give me your cure for being sad. Play me some music. Be like David in the Bible playing to calm King Saul.'

Adele smiled and walked over to the Steinway. She looked towards the window wondering what to play and then she looked, smiling, towards Khalim Said. She saw Gabriella smile as she played and sang softly, *'J'attendrai. Le jour et la nuit j'attendrai toujours . . . ton retour . . . '* When she finished, Khalim walked over and kissed the top of her head.

As Rennie walked back with her to the gallery she tucked her arm in his. 'I wonder why Khalim is so defensive with you.'

'Is he?'

'In all the time I've known him he's never talked about Arab affairs. Not even Arab art. But both times with you he's got wound up about it all.'

'I hope it's not me.'

'You certainly didn't start it. Maybe it's because you're British.'

'You're British too.'

She laughed. 'But I'm only a woman.'

She waited for him to agree but he didn't respond. As they stood at her door she said, 'When you want some company, just pop in. Anytime.'

'That's very kind of you. I will.'

She smiled at the formal schoolboyish response, kissed him on the cheek and let herself in to her flat.

It was drizzling as he walked over the bridge into War-moesstraat. He wondered if the girl would still be there.

As he opened the door she was standing there with the man. She was wearing only her skirt and the man's hand was between her legs. He saw the thin piece of cord and the syringe on the table. As he closed the door the man turned from the girl, hands on hips, his chin thrust out aggressively. He was in his middle-forties with a shaven head. Tall and heavily built with a black moustache that made him look faintly Victorian. Rennie guessed from the look of him that he was a Turk.

The man said, 'What you fuckin' here, mister?'

Rennie opened the door behind him, pointing as he said quietly, 'Get out.'

The man flexed his biceps and grinned as he said, 'You wanna try me to go, man?' And when Rennie didn't answer the man lurched forward, his right arm reaching out to Rennie's face with his thick fingers splayed apart. Rennie kicked him hard between his legs, and as the man's heavy body bent over, Rennie's knee smashed up under his jaw. He fell heavily, one hand clutching for support from the table and then the room shook as his body hit the floor. The girl was cowering against the wall, one hand to her face as she watched Rennie open the door and drag the man's body to the landing outside.

His face was white with anger as he walked back to the table and picked up the syringe. He heard the girl cry out as he thrust the needle deep into the man's big backside before he lifted him onto his shoulder and walked down the stairs, the man's feet banging on each stair until they reached the hall. Rennie opened the front door and shoved the man's body into the cobbled street.

The girl was sitting at the table, her whole body shaking as she looked at him. Her voice quavered as she said, 'That was a terrible thing to do.'

Rennie frowned. 'What thing?'

'All of it. Especially the syringe.'

'Who was he?'

'His name's Franco. He's a Turk.'

'A friend of yours?'

She sighed. 'No. He's just a pusher.'

'What does he deal in?'

'Anything. Everything.'

Rennie reached out for the small plastic envelope, and licked his finger before touching the off-white powder and bringing it to the tip of his tongue. It was cocaine.

'How much did you pay for this?'

She shrugged. 'I hadn't paid him.' She looked at his face.

'Why were you so . . . violent with him?'

'Me? For God's sake. It was he who started the violence. He probably isn't used to people who hit back. He's a bully, girl. A thug.'

'But you did it so . . .' She shrugged. '. . . clinically. Smoothly.'

Rennie shrugged. 'What did you want? An exhibition bout?'

'You must be terribly strong.'

'You could have done that, my dear. Never wait for a man to grab you. Kick him hard in the groin and the police can do the rest.'

'But the syringe.'

'He's got to learn his lesson, girl. We all have to. Pushing drugs is a dangerous game. And the danger's not always on the side of the victims. It happens both ways. You'd better put your sweater on and make us some coffee.'

'Don't I get taught a lesson too.'

Rennie pulled out the rickety chair and sat down at the table, his arms folded as he leaned back looking at the girl. 'What is it you want? One more lecture on the stupidity of taking drugs? You must have had plenty of those already. And it obviously hasn't convinced you, has it?'

'It isn't like you think.'

'Tell me what it's like.'

She sighed. 'It's an escape. An escape from the world. Money and power and corruption. Politicians, govern-ments, police – all the people who pressure people into doing what *they* want.'

'But if you didn't have law and order you'd have anarchy. The thugs like Franco would take over and the weak would go to the wall.'

'You mean people like me?'

'Yes. But not just you. Most people are weak in the face of threats and violence.'

'You're not weak.'

'Maybe not. It's easier for a man. And I've sorted out what I believe in. How I'm going to be – you haven't done that yet. But you will.'

'What makes you think that?'

'I know you will. I can tell.'

'Are you married?'

'Divorced.'

'Any children?'

'Yes. Two girls.'

'They're very lucky.'

'Why?'

She sighed. 'You don't agree with me but you don't put me down. At least you listen. And you're encouraging. You're the only person who's ever said anything encouraging or hopeful about me. My father thinks I'm disgusting. He wouldn't have me in the house.'

'He's just not very mature. That's all.'

'Oh he is. He's a very important man in our area. Very successful businessman with his own business. Big house, heated pool and all the trimmings.'

Rennie smiled. 'None of that makes him mature. Some of the most childish men I know are successful businessmen and stinking rich.'

'What's your job?'

'I work for a firm of lawyers as an investigator.'

'What are you doing in Amsterdam?'

He shrugged. 'Looking for someone.'

'Why are you in this dump? Why not a four-star hotel?'

'You don't find missing people in four-star hotels, my dear.'

'Do you want me to leave?'

'Do you want to?'

'No. I like it here.'

'Why?'

She smiled. 'I feel safe here with you.' She paused. 'I won't be a nuisance.'

'OK. We do a deal. You stay and you keep the place a bit tidy.'

'No rules? No regulations?'

'No. No rules, kid. Just relax.' As he stood up he reached inside his jacket and brought out a bundle of Dutch currency. 'We need to stock up. Get what you think we'll need for the next week. Can you cook?'

'I've never tried.'

'Buy a cookbook and start learning.'

She smiled as she stood up unsteadily, and as she passed his chair on her way to the bedroom her hand lightly touched his shoulder.

Back at the Prinsengracht apartment Rennie was reading through Jan Branders's report on the daily routines of the Said family when the phone rang. It was Paynter calling from the consulate.

'Just had an interesting call from London, Johnny. The Syrian embassy phoned the Law Society and asked for the name of a firm of solicitors big enough to have their own investigator. They were given four names. All four of them were contacted by the embassy and in each case they asked specifically if they had an investigator named John Rennie. There were broad hints that they might be putting business to whatever firm he worked for.'

'Did Langridge cover for me OK?'

'Of course. His clerk had been well briefed and so had he. And he's done it for us before.' Paynter laughed. 'Spoke highly of your talents and experience and said you were overseas at the moment looking for a missing person on behalf of one of their clients.'

'That must have been instigated by Khalim.'

'Yes. So much for him not wanting to be involved too deeply.'

'Thanks for letting me know.'

'There was another query from Finance. Do you want to add a voluntary contribution to your pension scheme? They've made some new deal with the insurance company so that you can increase your pension by a separate policy funded by you. Let them know sometime if you're interested. There's some bumph on the way to you.'

'I'll drop them a note when I've seen it.'

'Cheers.'

'Bye.'

Chapter 13

MOST DAYS Rennie paid brief visits to the rooms at Warmoesstraat. He tried different routes and timed them carefully. The girl seemed more relaxed and she talked to him about her family. Her father sounded a bit of a tyrant but her mother and sister sounded quite normal. She didn't try to blame her father or anyone else for her wayward behaviour and there was obviously a quite strong character underneath the hippie front. He wondered what he would do if Beth or young Mary turned out like this girl. Not that he expected them to, but these were funny times, especially for young people. He hoped that he'd be more constructive than the girl's father had been and he hoped that there would be somebody around who might bother to look for the virtues in his small girls.

On that particular day they had talked late into the night and his walk back to Prinsengracht was even less inviting than a night in the ramshackle chair.

It was five o'clock when Rennie finally gave up trying to sleep. He let himself out quietly and walked through the almost empty streets back to the Prinsengracht. It was going to be a warm day and already there were clouds of midges dancing over the canals. He slept until nine o'clock and lay in the warm bath for half an hour listening to Radio 4 on long-wave. London seemed far away.

As he sipped his second cup of coffee the door-bell rang. The three short and one long rings that Jan Branders had told him to use at his place. He tied his bath-robe as he walked to the door.

Jan Branders was standing there, unshaven and red-eyed. There was a bloody bandage around his right hand

and Rennie said quietly, 'Come in.' He could see the pain on Branders's face as he slumped down into the nearest armchair.

'What have you done to your hand?'

'Got it cut.'

'Have you seen a doctor?'

Branders shook his head.

'Who bandaged it up?'

'One of the girls.'

Rennie reached for the bandaged hand. There was a big area of dark, dried blood, but the stain on the palm was wet and bright red in the centre. The bandage had been fastened with a gilt safety-pin. As he peeled off the bandage he saw the wound. It was a deep knife cut from the base of the thumb right across the palm. It was deep and gaping, and the white glint of bone showed through in several places. He looked up at Branders's face. His eyes were closed and his brown skin was grey.

'You need a doctor, Jan,' he said quietly but firmly. 'You need stitches in this. I'll get a taxi and go with you.'

'I gotta talk with you first. You got big trouble.'

'We'll talk later. Just sit there while I get dressed.'

Before he dressed Rennie checked the Yellow Pages and called a taxi. As he dressed hurriedly he called out.

'Where's the nearest doctor, d'you know, Jan?'

'Not in town. They tell the *politie*.'

'Is there a doctor on the canals?'

'Yes.'

'We'll go there.' The door-bell rang and he called out. 'I'll answer it – don't move.'

Branders gave the taxi-driver an address and the man didn't look any too happy. But ten minutes later he pulled up outside a house on the Ouderzijds Voorburgwal. There was a girl in a white bra and panties already sitting in the window. Jan pointed at the stone steps and Rennie paid off the driver and got Branders unsteadily up the steps, leaving a trail of blood spots as they went. At the top of the steps Jan pressed the middle button of three with his closed fist and seconds later the door clicked open.

On the first floor the door was open and a Chinese man

stood waiting for them to go in. Inside the small room Jan spoke to him in Dutch and the man nodded as he looked at the hand, holding it gently. Then he took Branders behind a green curtain.

Twenty minutes later Branders came out, looking less pale and with his hand properly bandaged. The doctor said slowly to Rennie, 'To keep warm. Not use for three days. Have given injection of iron for loss of blood.'

Rennie nodded and when he took out a bundle of notes the old man smiled and waved it aside. Rennie looked at Branders.

'Can you walk with me to your place?'

'I'm OK now, Johnny. We better talk together. Have coffees.'

'Whatever you want, Jan.'

The old man watched them go slowly down the stairs and out onto the street.

Five minutes later they were sitting at a table in the sleazy coffeeshop where they had first met. Branders looked at Rennie for a long time before he spoke.

'These mens who got your man. The Arab is a bad man. Real bad.' He took a deep breath. 'He killed my man when he go back. Cut out his tongue alive. Cut off his dick and put in his mouth. Cut open his belly and let him die slow.'

'How do you know this, Jan?'

'One of the Arab's men was scared and came back to tell me. They send killer to get him. I send him out of Netherlands.'

'How did you get cut?'

'When he find him gone he come for me.'

'Where is he now?'

'He drinking canal water. Was very bad for his health.'

'What's happening at the boat?'

'They make your man write. Every day they beat him up and afterwards he write.' Branders glanced quickly around the coffeeshop and lowered his voice. 'Whatever you are doing with those Arab . . . that Arab . . . you not trust him. He laugh at your people. Make jokes of the English. He say too much of gentlemans. You think is games but is war. All that he say them. Surinam men real scared of him.

103

They do all he say – Jesus . . .' Branders's mouth grimaced with pain and he closed his eyes until the spasm of pain had passed.

'You know where the boat is, don't you?'

'OK. I know.'

'Tell me.'

'They kill your man if anyone find them. The Arab say so. They cut his throat and watched him bleed to death like sacrificial sheep.'

'Tell me, Jan. Where is it?'

'You heard of Lóosdrechtse lake?'

'No. Where is it?'

'Is big big lake north of Utrecht. The boat is on Hilversum canal. Just east of village called Vreeland. Is windmill on canal. Three boats together north of windmill. Their boat is middle boat. Big, heavy canal boat. Name of *Het Vlaamsche Leeuw*.'

'What's that mean?'

'Is meaning *The Flemish Lion*. Is a Belgian boat.'

'They could move it somewhere else.'

'No. I ask. Is no engine. And not safe to move even with tractor or horses.'

'When you say he jokes about the English what does he joke about?'

'He say you don' understand Arabs. You make some deal but when you do your part they not do for their bargain.'

'You're sure that's what he means?'

'Quite, quite sure. Hundert pro cent.'

'Thanks for telling me.'

Branders shook his head slowly. 'Go home, Johnny. Is bad scene for you here.'

'You know me better than that, Jan. Just let me keep the room and we're all square. No obligations either side. OK?'

'OK for me. You still my buddy.'

'Let me walk to your place with you.'

'No. I got business to talk here.' He smiled. 'Nice clean business of white powder and brown paradise for pipe-smokers.'

Rennie stood up. 'Thanks, Jan. And if you ever need me just phone the consulate. Ask for Lambert, he'll put you in touch.'

Branders nodded and signalled to the man behind the counter for more coffee.

Almost without thinking Rennie walked back slowly to the room in Warmoesstraat. As he turned the key in the lock and pushed open the door he saw a man sitting at the table. A well-dressed man in his fifties.

Chapter 14

AS RENNIE walked in and closed the door the man stood up.

'I guess you must be Rennie. John Rennie.'

'Who are you?'

'My name's de Vries. Johan de Vries.'

'Who let you in?'

'My daughter let me in.'

'I see. You're Joanna's father?'

'Indeed I am.'

'Where is she?'

'I don't know. She was angry at me coming here. Angry that I had found out where she was holed-up. She walked out on me.'

'Sit down, Mr de Vries,' Rennie said amiably. 'No need to stand. Would you like a cup of coffee?'

'You're a pretty cool customer, Rennie. Not what I expected, I might say.'

Rennie sat down facing de Vries. 'What were you expecting, Mr de Vries?'

'Somebody younger, I guess. One of those long-haired bums she's always hung around with.'

'And why are you still here?'

'Don't try and bluff me, Rennie. I know your kind. You may be a bit smoother than the others but you're all tarred with the same brush. Drugs, sex, crime, you don't deceive me.'

Rennie said quietly, 'I think you'd better leave, Mr de Vries, or you might not like being thrown out into the street in broad daylight.'

'You lay a hand on me, my friend, and I'll have you in jail

in an hour.'

Rennie looked at the man's flushed face. He was a pathetic figure. A bluffer as well as a tyrant. But he was a sad figure at the same time. He wanted to protect his daughter from the unknown forces that he was sure her life implied. To him it wasn't a question of her loneliness or helplessness but a fantasy of sexual orgies laced with drugs. And the crime that supplied the money to buy the drugs. Rennie said quietly, 'What made you come to see her?'

'You picked her up in the street when she was with some squatters, didn't you?'

'That's one way of putting it. Go on.'

'One of those kids was from our town. He told me she was facing charges as a drug-peddlar and she'd signed a statement saying she had no money to defend herself. I phoned our embassy in The Hague and they put me in touch with the consul here in Amsterdam. He suggested I appoint a lawyer to defend her. I wanted to talk with her and see if I was wasting my time and money again.'

'How did you find her?'

'The kid told me where they'd been squatting and he saw her go off with you. Right opposite, he said. And he was right.'

'And what are you going to do now, Mr de Vries?'

'I've told her she's brought shame on her whole family. It's time she faced up to life.'

'What does that mean exactly – "face up to life"?'

'When she's served her sentence she'd better get back to the States and start earning a living like everybody else has to do. I'd been working for two, three years by the time I was her age. Contributing to the family funds. Going to classes at night. Not bumming around like some kid from the wrong side of the tracks.'

'You said that to her?'

'I certainly did.'

'More or less those words?'

'Exactly those words.'

Rennie looked at the man's angry face. 'Not the best way of solving the problem, if you don't mind me saying so.'

'And what would you do if you were me, Mr Rennie?'

'If you mean what would I do if I was her father then I'd use my influence with the American consul here in Amsterdam and the embassy in The Hague and get the charge withdrawn. That's what I'd do first anyway.'

'And would it work? Would the authorities here play ball?'

'Despite what people say, drug peddling is a serious charge in this city, but I'm sure they wouldn't get a conviction. I'd guess I'd want to talk to the public prosecutor if she was my daughter.'

'You said you'd do that first. What else would you do?'

Rennie looked at de Vries as he spoke. 'I'd make her an allowance so that she's not totally dependent on other people. And I'd try to convince her that I loved her just as much as I love her kid sister.'

'She's talked to you about her family?'

'Yes. A lot.'

'And you see me as a hard-nosed father who's thrown her out and left her destitute, eh?'

'No. Let me be frank, Mr de Vries. I don't like you, and I don't like your attitude, and I'm not surprised that your daughter left home. I see you as a man who was brought up with a set of rules governing relationships and behaviour. Good rules. Nothing wrong with the rules. Except that they have to be applied with a lot of love and affection.' Rennie paused. 'I guess you are a very busy man, Mr de Vries. Maybe your younger daughter was easier to deal with, more amenable. And maybe you'd never been told what to do if someone you loved wouldn't go along with the rules. Not just your rules but any rules.'

De Vries looked at Rennie intently. 'You're an odd kind of man, Mr Rennie.'

Dr Vries waited for Rennie to ask him why he thought he was odd but Rennie didn't respond. He wasn't interested in what de Vries thought of him.

De Vries said, 'I suppose you sleep with my daughter?'

'You must suppose what you want, mister.'

'Do you sleep with her?'

'You're not entitled to ask me that, Mr de Vries. You gave up that right a couple of years back. Maybe even before. But I understand why you ask so I'll tell you. No. I don't sleep with your daughter, and I never have done.'

'Why answer me if you think I'm not entitled to ask?'

'Because you're wondering if you should take my advice about what to do. If I sleep with her you can dismiss the advice as coming from an interested party. A party with an axe to grind. Without that you've got to at least consider what I said. And maybe change your whole thinking about your daughter.'

'I heard from several people who've been over here and come back home that she'd been sleeping around.'

'Did they also tell you she was desperately lost and unhappy despite her tough front?'

'She was arrogant enough when she was speaking to me.'

'She's twenty, nearly twenty-one, and she hates being ordered about by anybody. She knows that she only has to do what you say, knuckle under, and she can be back in the big house with the servants and the money and all the rest of it. So why doesn't she just give in?'

'That's what I ask myself.'

'And?'

'And what?'

'And what's your answer? Why doesn't she just give up?'

'I guess she's stubborn and stupid. She doesn't know what the real world is all about.'

'How old are you, Mr de Vries?'

'I'm fifty-seven.'

'Let me tell you something, Mr de Vries. Your girl Joanna knows more about what the real world is like than you do.' Rennie paused. 'Maybe more than you'll ever know,' he said quietly.

'You say that because you're on her side. You believe in the rubbish she believes in. Anti-everything that makes society work.'

Rennie shifted in his chair and stared back at de Vries with barely concealed anger. 'You know nothing about my views. In fact I go along with most of your views. The only difference is that I accept that most other people don't share them. You want to fight your own daughter – beat her into submission. Not by argument but by blackmail. Moral blackmail. No home, no mother, no family, no money – unless you toe your dear daddy's line. You're as bad as the drug pushers, Mr de Vries. You want a daughter of twenty who thinks like a mature man. Heaven help her.'

Rennie stood up and de Vries stood up too. Slowly and uncertainly. And as they stood facing one another de Vries said softly, 'I loathe you, Rennie. I hate your guts.' He paused. 'But I'll do what you say.'

'You never asked me if she was innocent of the drug-pushing charge, did you?'

'No.'

'You assumed she was guilty?'

'I assumed that the authorities wouldn't have charged her unless they had convincing evidence.'

'That shows how little you know of the real world, mister. Your daughter's never pushed a speck of any drug in her life.'

'How do you know?'

'Because I asked her.'

'And you believed her?'

'What a father.' Rennie shook his head slowly. 'God help her. She's mixed up and unhappy but I'll tell you this . . . she's one of the most honest people I've ever met. I'd bet my last dollar that you tell more lies in business in a week than she's ever told in her life. No wonder she's mixed up.'

De Vries opened his mouth to speak, changed his mind and stood up, walking to the door, banging it behind him without looking back.

It was almost midnight when she came back. He said nothing about her father but for once she offered to make the coffee. He heard her humming softly to herself as she waited for the water to boil. It was one of the tunes the girls liked. From some film. Something about 'Over the rainbow'.

As she put the coffee in front of him and sat down she was smiling and it was the first time he'd ever seen her smile genuinely. She laughed as she said, 'I understand you had a confrontation with my father.'

'How did you know?'

'I went to the Amstel where he's staying. I apologised for

111

what I said to him earlier.'

'Good girl. Never lose your temper. If you're in the right you don't need to. If you're in the wrong you can't afford to.'

She smiled. 'And here endeth the second lesson. You certainly made an impression. Purple Hearts and Congressional medals barely good enough.' She reached out and put her hand on his. 'You're a good man, Johnny Rennie. I hope that somebody's being good to you.'

Rennie looked at his watch. 'Time you were in bed, honey. It's tomorrow already.'

The next morning he was awake early, stiff from his night in the uncomfortable chair, thinking instead of sleeping. Thinking of what Jan Branders had told him. Trying not to think of what it meant he had to do.

He made breakfast, knocked on the bedroom door and when they had eaten he took her for a walk in the sun.

He bought her an ice-cream cone and they sat on a bench in the sunshine in the small square. Now that she was eating and resting, her face and her body had already changed. The pallor and the brown patches under her eyes had gone and her face was beginning to fill out. She looked younger now and the big heavy-lidded blue eyes were clear and beautiful. Her hands still trembled as she held the ice-cream but it was only her hands. She turned to look at him, smiling.

'You still think I'm an anarchist?'

'You are, Joanna. Not a cartoon one with a bomb in your hand and a striped jersey, but an anarchist all the same.'

'I don't want to change anything. I just don't want to be part of it myself.'

'Part of what?'

'A corrupt society.'

'It's a tough world, kid. Always was and always will be.'

'But why should it be? Why should people be so rotten?'

Rennie laughed softly. 'Who've you got in mind this time?'

She sighed. 'You know what I mean.'

'Tell me.'

'Why do politicians have to be corrupt? Why do educated men spend their energies selling people rubbish they don't need? Why don't people care about the losers? Why are money and success the only things that matter?'

'As long as you recognise that that's what it's like, you won't get hooked. You're much the same as them anyway.'

'How on earth do you make that out?'

'Don't sound so surprised. They're turned on by power and money and you're turned on by grass and coke. What's the difference?'

'What I do doesn't hurt anyone but me.'

'When a politician gets a pay-off for giving a construction job to an old friend that's what he says to himself. Somebody's got to build the road so why not old Joe? And don't kid yourself that taking drugs doesn't hurt anyone but you. It does and you know it.'

'And the people who advertise and sell junk we don't need?'

'What junk for instance?'

'Junk food. Dish-washers, stupid cosmetics.'

'They sell junk food because people are busy at their jobs and haven't got time to prepare old-fashioned food. That's why they need dish-washers too. To save time.'

'Save time to do what?'

'Go to ball-games, swim, play with their kids.'

'You're a good arguer, Johnny Rennie. I wish I knew how to argue back. But winning an argument doesn't mean you're right. It just means you're a good arguer.'

'Tell me what you'd really like for yourself.'

She looked up at the sun and then at the children by the fountain.

'I'd like to live somewhere quiet. A small farm. Just getting by. Doing nobody any harm. Just growing good food for people to eat.'

'I'd say your old man would stake you to that if he thought it would make you happy.'

She leaned towards him, smiling. 'How did you make him change his mind about me and like me?'

'He always liked you. Loved you in his own way. But

suddenly his pet lamb turned into a carnivore and snarled at him. He didn't know what to do. Didn't want to shoot it so he chained it up. Which made it worse. I'd guess he's shed a lot of tears about you in his time.'

'But he doesn't love me properly or he wouldn't have thrown me out.'

Rennie looked at his watch. 'Time to get back, honey. I'll see you in a couple of days. How are our housekeeping funds?'

'I've got enough for at least two weeks.'

Rennie stood up, reached for her hand and pulled her gently to her feet. She slid her arm in his as they walked back to the rooms.

He opened the shutters on the window and then looked out on the cobbled street and over to where the sun was setting behind the church tower. When he turned she was looking at him and she said softly, 'Don't you ever have any doubts, Johnny?'

'About what?'

'About life. How to think. How to behave. How to react to other people.'

'No. I just do what I think is right.'

'How do you decide what's right?'

'I don't decide. I just know. You know too. Just as well as I do.'

'So why am I like I am?'

Rennie shrugged. 'You wanted to make sure that the wrong way wasn't more fun.' He paused. 'You can't kid either of us that squatting in an Amsterdam alley is the equivalent of that quiet life in the country you talked about.' He smiled. 'But you'll be OK, kid, don't worry. You'll work it out.'

'How do you know?'

'You're too bright to want to end up in the gutter.'

'What should I do next?'

'Sit down and think. About the world and about your-self.' He paused. 'And think, perhaps, of looking at England. It's got advantages for a girl like you. The lan-guage and the people. The Dutch are tolerant but in a different sort of way. Anyway. Think about it.'

'Would you do something to help me?'

'Yes.'

'You didn't ask what it was.'

'Tell me.'

'My father wants to apologise to you. He asked if you'll see him in the Amstel tomorrow morning before he leaves. He said he'd stay in in case you can.'

'I'll see what I can do.'

She walked over to him and looked up at his face. 'When will you be coming back here?'

'I'm not sure. A couple of days maybe.'

'It's better when you're here. I get lonely when you're not here. You're so different. You're sane and – I don't know – honest.'

'Don't depend on me, girl. Just stand on your own two feet. Be independent.' Impulsively he kissed her forehead. 'I'll be back.'

She was still standing there as he closed the door behind him and clattered down the wooden stairs.

De Vries had a luxury suite at the Amstel Hotel and when Rennie gave his name in at reception he was expected and escorted to the second floor immediately.

The American was standing looking out of the window as Rennie walked in and he turned quickly.

'I'm grateful to you for coming, Mr Rennie. A coffee or a drink?' De Vries's hand hovered over the service bell but Rennie shook his head.

'Do sit down, Mr Rennie. Perhaps you wouldn't object to me calling you Johnny?' De Vries had got his confidence back and he didn't wait for an answer. He sat down facing Rennie. 'You know, Johnny, I owe you an apology. I jumped to conclusions. The wrong conclusions. I wanted the chance to apologise.'

'Don't worry, Mr de Vries. You were very worried about your daughter's situation.'

'Let me say I followed your advice. The charges have been withdrawn and I gather they weren't going to take them further anyway. But it's not just an apology I owe you. I want to thank you for what you've done for my daughter. She was very angry when I told her my suspicions.' He paused. 'I wish that she felt about me as she does about you.'

Rennie shrugged. 'She probably will. Just give her time.'

'You're a very unusual man, Mr Rennie – Johnny. You gave a young girl shelter and food and asked nothing in return. You don't know what an effect it has had on that girl. She's seen a man, a good-looking man, an attractive active man who's got standards. She told me about her talks with you. That you've never criticised her crazy way of life or the stupid things she does. I'm afraid I wasn't wise enough to take that attitude.' He shrugged. 'But that's water under the bridge now. She doesn't admit it but she's beginning to change her thinking. I can tell. Still anti-everything but calm about it.' De Vries gave an embarrassed shrug. 'So. I want to ask if there's anything I can do to repay you. To show my thanks.'

'Are you friends with one another now?'

'She's very cautious but on my side we're friends.'

'Will she be able to write home to her mother and sister?'

'I've told her she can be just how she wants to be and if some time she wanted to come home then there'd be the fattest calf on the spit that Pittsburgh's ever seen. No explanations. No judgements on my part. I'd just love to see her back.'

'Well that's payment enough for me, Mr de Vries.'

'That's not really what I meant – but let me say this – if there's ever a good turn you need, Johnny, I'd be flattered if you turned to me. I've learned my lesson and I'm grateful. You've got a permanent invitation and welcome at my house.'

'Well, thank you and congratulations. I'm glad it's turned out well for both of you. I'll keep an eye on her while I'm around.'

De Vries walked with him down to the hotel foyer and shook his hand enthusiastically.

Chapter 15

HE PHONED London and Paynter agreed to a meeting, but Paynter didn't want the meeting in his office. He seemed uncertain and on edge and finally he opted for the old familiar meeting-place – a bench in St James's Park.

They sat opposite the island and Paynter was affecting an interest in the ducks. Rennie said quietly, 'What do you want me to do?'

'You've eliminated the idea of offering him money, I gather.'

'He's got more money than the total SIS budget for the next ten years.'

'I've never met a rich man who wasn't greedy for more, Johnny.'

'Not Khalim Said, I assure you.'

'What about physical pressure? You grab him and give him the works.'

'The people holding Mason wouldn't give a damn whatever we did to Said.'

'Would he himself?'

Rennie shrugged. 'He's not hero material if that's what you mean. But it would be pointless. He could scream his head off and the others wouldn't give a damn.'

'So what are we left with?'

'You tell me.'

'You know what we have to go for as well as I do.'

'So don't beat around the bush, tell me what you want me to do.'

'We'll have to lift his kids, put pressure on him that way, so that he uses his influence on the higher-up Arabs who are backing these people.'

'Or I could move in on the gang holding Mason and wipe them out. Get Mason and whatever documents they've got at the same time.'

'You know that isn't a runner. Apart from the diplomatic outcry they could have copies of Mason's stuff lodged somewhere else.'

Rennie shrugged. 'So, like I said originally, we swear that the documents are fakes.'

'And every journalist in London clamouring for an interview with Mason.'

'Threaten him with the Official Secrets Act.'

'He'd cave in under the pressure like he has with the kidnappers.'

'So let me deal with Mason on the spot. We can say that he got in the crossfire or they killed him so we couldn't prove they were faked.'

'Crossfire,' Paynter rasped. 'There ain't gonna be any crossfire, Johnny. The whole point of what we've been doing is to keep it quiet.'

Rennie shrugged, putting his hand on his thighs preparatory to standing up. 'OK. I'll take the children. But I'll need a few days to work out a plan.'

Paynter half-smiled. 'You mean you haven't already worked it out?'

Rennie sighed. 'Yes. But I need to go over it again.' He stood up. 'Anything else while I'm over here?'

'No.' Paynter stood up too, not looking at Rennie as he said quietly, 'I'll see that you get appropriate recognition when this is over, Johnny. You can rely on that.'

'I'll walk back with you and get a pool car to take me to the airport.'

Paynter grinned and patted Rennie's shoulder. 'No way. We'll get a taxi in Horse Guards. And a pool car can take you to Gatwick. Never walk when you can ride. That's the one bit of training I always remember.'

Rennie sat with his small hold-all at a table by the self-service counter at Gatwick, and emptied two packets of sugar into his coffee.

118

As he sipped the hot sweet mixture he looked at the people in the cafeteria. Working people, families on their way to Majorca and Benidorm. Construction workers and oil-men on their way back to the Gulf. A handful of businessmen clutching briefcases as they ate stale sausage rolls. Infrequent travellers or they'd have fixed themselves up in one of the so-called VIP lounges. He wondered if they valued their hum-drum routine lives where their only worries were the mortgage, their children's 'O' levels and keeping their jobs.

Not that he envied them their peaceful pursuits, he would have hated to live their lives. But he wondered what they would think if they knew about the things he did. They wouldn't envy him. They probably wouldn't even vaguely understand. They didn't care about the country they lived in. They were fond of the royals in the same way that they idolised a football team or some scruffy pop group. They probably couldn't name two members of the Cabinet or even their own Member of Parliament. They didn't believe in a God so why should they believe in anything? They hadn't always been like that, but nowadays they relied on the State for everything. But they didn't value what was done for them. It was always 'their' responsibility to protect them and care for them. And if they could avoid paying the taxes that it cost to cosset them they did it without a moment's feeling of guilt. Jack Kennedy had been right when he said, 'Ask not what your country can do for you but what you can do for your country.' Never for a moment did Rennie's thoughts extend as far as questioning the fact that what he was doing for his country at the moment was planning the cold-blooded kidnapping of two small children. It was something they wanted him to do. The people who cared for Britain. The people who knew what had to be done.

He remembered that he hadn't asked Paynter to send Ryan over and he walked to a call-box and left a message for Paynter.

Chapter 16

RYAN FLEW in the next day and Rennie put him up in the spare bedroom, but they worked all day and through most of the night. Ryan's team were specialists at dealing with kidnap incidents. Ryan himself was both tough and intelligent. The four other members of his team included an expert car-driver and a psychologist. Ryan and his men spent their whole time studying kidnappings and their perpetrators whether the objectives were merely ransoms or political. They were consulted by the police and the military, and from time to time they advised friendly governments faced with a political kidnapping.

Rennie took him to see the outside of the Said apartment and Ryan had paced out the surrounding streets and alleyways. Back at the Prinsengracht he had made Rennie describe everything that he could recall of the layout and furnishings of the place.

For an hour Ryan went carefully through Jan Branders's report on the Said family's daily routine. By mid-afternoon he was ready to talk, the street maps laid out on the table in front of him.

'Who did this report on the family's movements, Johnny?'

Rennie shrugged. 'A friend of mine.'

'Wouldn't make "O" level English, whoever he is.'

'How's your Taki Taki?'

'What the hell's that?'

'It's his language. He's Surinamese.'

'Is he reliable?'

'He's reliable enough but he's not a trained observer.'

'It's the times that matter to me. Will those be accurate?'

'Yes. They're local times of course, not GMT.'

'The best time to pick up those children is in the morning when the car comes to take them to school. The school will assume they're not coming and that could give us all day before the balloon goes up.' Ryan paused. 'And that brings me to the main question. Will Said bring in the Dutch police, d'you reckon?'

'It's hard to say. My guess is that he won't. Not at first anyway. He'll be scared of prejudicing his diplomatic status here if anything comes out about what he's been involved in. But he's very fond of his children. That might make him panic and call in the police.'

'So we pick up the two kids. Stash them away. Contact him. Tell him the only way he'll get them back is for Mason to be released unharmed. What about a time limit?'

'What do you think? A week?'

'Not longer anyway. These things begin to start falling apart after four or five days no matter how well planned they are.'

'It must seem odd for you, to be on the other side for once.'

'Not really. I always have to think as if I were on the other side when we're acting against them. And interrogating them afterwards you learn a lot about what they were thinking and the effect your own moves had on them at the time.'

'Is this going to be tougher or easier than the usual kidnappings?'

'Picking them up should be easy. Keeping them under wraps shouldn't be difficult unless the police are drawn in and the media get hold of it. This is a small country. Everybody knows everybody. And when you're dealing with fanatics you can't rely on previous experience.'

Rennie nodded. 'We've got two lots of fanatics here. The psychopath who's actually holding Mason, and the lunatics back in Damascus who are supposed to be in charge. Will the Arab on the boat do what Khalim Said tells him to do? Will he do what even his masters tell him to do? It's going to be tricky.'

Ryan half-smiled. 'I'm afraid that's going to be your

problem, Johnny. I'm only responsible for the washing up.'

'When can you start?'

'I'll move out of here tomorrow and find myself a place. I'll want a day's observation myself and then I'll get my chaps over and brief them. Say four days from today, five at the worst.'

'The sooner the better, Pat. It must be getting a bit hairy on that boat.'

'OK. I'll phone Paynter from the consulate now and get my chaps over tonight. I'll find them a place outside Amsterdam while I'm waiting.'

'Do you need funds?'

'No. We've got our own sources over here already. Paynter fixed that yesterday.' Ryan stood up, stretching his arms. 'I'll move out myself tomorrow if you can put up with me tonight.'

'You're welcome to use this place any time you want, Pat. You know that.'

'See you later then.' As Ryan walked to the door he turned. 'Is it OK to give Lambert this address and the telephone number?'

'He's got them already.'

Ryan nodded, looked at his watch and closed the door quietly behind him.

Ryan came back just after eight that evening. He didn't say much about what he'd been doing but Rennie gathered that he'd spoken to Paynter and had already found a place for his team well out of the city.

As they sat at the table drinking coffee Ryan said, 'That was wonderful smoked salmon, Johnny. I must take some back with me when this caper's over.'

'How's that beautiful wife of yours?'

'She's fine. Wouldn't approve of this little lot though.'

'Why not?'

Ryan shrugged. 'Not many women would go along with kidnapping kids.'

'Do you know Mason?'

'I've met him a time or two. Nice enough chap but a bit

wet I thought.'

'Have you met his wife?'

'No. I've seen a photograph. A real cracker.'

'You know they're splitting up? Divorce and all that.'

'No. I hadn't heard.' He shrugged. 'Happens to the best in this game.'

'Khalim Said, the children's father, went to Paris quite deliberately intending to screw Mason's wife just to check that he was SIS and a suitable guy for them to kidnap.'

Ryan laughed. 'An original story anyway. Mind you, she looked a bit of a sex-pot in the photo.'

'It wasn't difficult to get her into bed but in case you had doubts you might as well know that Said isn't some innocent bystander. He's asked for it. And he's the go-between for the Arabs.'

Ryan shook his head. 'I don't have any doubts. It's all the same to me, Johnny. I couldn't care less about what he's been up to.'

'We're going to need portable transceivers so that you and I can keep in touch.'

'My technical guy's bringing four pairs over, they'll be here in the morning.'

The phone rang and Rennie picked up the receiver.

'It's Paynter, Johnny. Can you hear me OK?'

'Yes. Loud and clear.'

'I had a message through about an hour ago from our friends in foreign parts. Looks like your Surinam chap was right, and they're going to renege. Not said it in so many words but strong indications that way. Tell your Irish friend there that the sooner he gets cracking the better. It's beginning to fall apart. OK?'

'Understood.'

He heard the click as Paynter hung up and as he replaced the receiver he said to Ryan, 'A message from Paynter. He's had a tip-off from our boys on the spot that the Arabs are going to renege on the deal. He asks that you act as soon as possible.' He paused. 'If they intend reneging they'll wipe out Mason before they pack it in.'

Ryan nodded. 'I'll pack my bags and meet my chaps in at Schiphol. They're coming in on a chartered plane from

Biggin Hill.' He stood up, leaning on the back of his chair. 'I'll send my guy round here about eleven tomorrow morning. He'll go over the portable with you in case it's one you don't know.'

At 5 a.m. the phone rang. It was Ryan, sounding very much awake.

'Johnny?'

'Yep.'

'Tomorrow's the day. There'll be no contact today from us to you so make the best of it because you'll be stuck in your place after that. Or somewhere we can always contact you. The equipment's coming your way about now, OK?'

'OK. Best of British.'

Ryan laughed softly and hung up.

Chapter 17

AS HE opened the door of the room he just stood there amazed. She was putting some flowers in a vase and she smiled as she saw the surprise on his face. The sleazy room had been transformed. The walls painted, the whole place cleaned, and pictures from magazines pinned up on a cork display board fastened to the wall.

She laughed. 'Don't overdo it. It's only a lick of paint.'

'It must have taken you ages.'

'One day and half one night. I never want to see another can of white paint in all my life. The cleaning down took most time. It hadn't been stripped since God knows when.'

As he closed the door he said, 'It's a marvellous job. Makes me want to move in right away.'

The blue eyes looked at his face and she said softly, 'I wish you would.' When she saw his indifference she became brisk again. 'Tea, coffee or hot chocolate?'

'Hot chocolate.'

As they drank from brand-new mugs she said, 'Where do you stay when you're not here?'

'Oh. Here and there. Nowhere special.'

'What do you do?'

'See the sights, look around.' He paused. 'And what have you been doing apart from painting and decorating?'

'Father gave me some money and I've been making a list of jobs I might like to have a go at.'

'Such as?'

'Nursing, social worker, probation officer, teacher . . .' She blushed. '. . . things like that.'

'You'd be good at any one of those. What's the next step?'

'Getting some training.'

'Here or in the States?'

'I thought I would have a last couple of months here in Amsterdam and go back home at the end of September.'

Rennie smiled. 'You know, I'm proud of you. You've really sorted yourself out. And quickly. Well done.'

'It's mostly been you.'

'Not me, girl. What makes you think that?'

'I don't really know. You believe in everything I hate. Governments, the Establishment, laws, rules, obeying . . . all that. But somehow it doesn't matter. All that matters is that you're so terribly honest. And you don't try and force people to think your way. You don't even try to persuade them. That's really something.'

'I'm going to take you for a nice lunch, so if you've got to fix anything fix it now.'

'Where are we going?'

'To the Schiller. Do you know it?'

'I've seen it from the outside. It looks nice.'

They walked from the restaurant to the Dam square and sat on the steps watching the crowds stroll by in the sunshine. An hour later he walked her back to Warmoesstraat, left her there and headed back to Prinsengracht. He was in bed by nine o'clock.

Chapter 18

GABRIELLA SAID clutched her dressing-gown around her with one hand and waved to the children with the other. The taxi-driver put the car in gear and drove off on the usual route to the school. When he eventually turned right into the narrow alley that led to the bridge he stopped and waited for the big Mercedes to come across the bridge. When it stopped he signalled to it to move aside so that he could pass. He was too intent on the blockage ahead of him to notice the man who came from behind.

As the man opened the car door the driver turned to curse him and only then did he see the gun. As he looked up the cotton-wool pad covered his mouth and nose. He was almost unconscious as he was dragged out and carried to the big Mercedes.

A man came from each rear door at the children. A hand over each mouth and a prick in the arm that they barely noticed.

The taxi engine was still running and one of the men swung it into the open gates by the old flour mill. By the time the taxi-driver had been dumped in his own car boot and the children pushed onto the back-seat of the Mercedes only two minuts had elapsed.

The big Merc continued over the last few feet of the bridge, turned towards the Central Station then south to Rembrandtsplein down Utrechtsestraat to Frederiksplein across to Westeinde. Then it was straight on to the Utrechtse bridge and the A2. As they passed the Over-amstel sports complex it was 9.20 a.m. Ryan glanced at his watch again as they turned west off the highway just before Breukelen. Four kilometres further on, the roadsign pointed north to Joostendam. The car bumped over the rutted road and turned into the open gate of the ramshackle farmhouse and stopped. Ryan could just see the sails of the distant windmill catching the sun.

At two o'clock the carpenter who rented one of the two garages in the old flour mill had phoned the traffic police to complain about the parked taxi that was stopping him from getting his car out of the garage.

The taxi was owned by a radio-taxi company and they sent one of their staff to bring it in. By the time he arrived the traffic police had discovered the unconscious driver in the boot of the taxi and had radioed the BAR who were on their way over.

Rennie's phone rang at 4 p.m. and when he picked it up Ryan's voice said quietly, 'Done. All OK. You can start.'

In the small bedroom Rennie turned the switch on the ICOM to transmit and tapped out the two-word code for Paynter to go ahead.

Khalim Said picked up the phone and spoke in Dutch but the reply was in English.

'Mr Khalim Said?'

'Yes.'

'Where are your children, Mr Said?'

'They're at school.'

'I'm afraid not, Mr Said. Your children are a long way from home. Would you like to see them again?'

'What do you mean. My children are . . .'

'Don't argue, Mr Said. Answer my question. Do you want to see your children again. Alive?'

Said felt the room revolving as he reached for a chair and sat down heavily.

'What is all this? I don't understand.'

'But you do, Mr Said, you have been talking to a friend of mine in London. About a Mr Mason, yes? A friend of my friend. And now I talk to you about your children. Would you like to make an exchange? There's not much time left.

If you go to the police, things could be very bad for your kids. Think about it, Mr Said.'

And the speaker hung up. Said dialled for the operator and asked them to trace the number of his caller.

'That's not possible, sir. We don't have records of numbers of dialled calls for incoming calls.'

Said tried to stand up, his legs shaking as his wife came into the room with a tray of coffee cups and cream. She put it down quickly and hurried over to him as he sat down weakly.

'What is it, love? What is it?' She saw the beads of perspiration on his face, his chest rising and falling rapidly. 'I'll call the doctor. Keep quite still.'

Said groaned. 'No. No. The children . . . don't.'

She smiled. 'The children are all right. They'll be on their way home now.'

He shook his head slowly, gasping as he said, 'They've taken them. Kidnapped them.'

She stood frozen but unbelieving. 'Don't say such things, Khalim.'

'They just phoned . . . said they had the children . . . my God, I don't believe it . . .' He looked at her, shaking his head as tears rolled slowly down his cheeks. '. . . but it's true.'

'And they demand money, yes? We pay them quickly. Tonight. Phone them back now. Say yes . . . whatever they want . . . we will give them.'

'Get me a brandy, Gabbie.'

He closed his eyes, not opening them until he had taken the first sip from the glass she put into his hand. As the brandy worked he drank the rest of the glass.

'Sit down, Gabbie. We've got to talk.'

She pulled up a gilt chair and reached for his hand. 'Stay calm, Khalim. Stay calm.'

'I'm helpless, Gabbie. As helpless as if I had ropes around me. They offer the children in exchange for a man. A man who is held prisoner by other people. People I don't control.'

'I don't understand, Khalim. What man? What other people?'

'The man is called Mason. He is an Englishman. The men who have him are Arabs under orders from Damascus.'

'Why do they have him?'

'They got hold of some high-technology war equipment made by the Israelis. They couldn't make it work. They kidnapped Mason so that his friends would show them how to use it.'

'But what has this got to do with you?'

'I acted as a go-between for them, passing their messages to Mason's friends in London and passing their replies back to Damascus.'

'But why you?'

'Because I speak English and understand the English. Because I have diplomatic status. Because they trust me.'

'Who is this Mason?'

He sighed heavily as he looked at her face. 'He's an English Secret Service man,'

For a moment she frowned and then her face was white with anger. 'You must be mad. You risk the safety of all your family for those madmen in Damascus. You sacrifice our children to make a piece of equipment work. Why? Why? Why did you have anything to do with it?'

His brown eyes pleaded as he looked at her face. 'They asked me, my love. I'm a Palestinian. They are my people. I had to do what I could.'

'You fool.' She whispered. 'You stupid, stupid fool. A few soft words of flattery and your family can be put at risk. What kind of man are you?'

'You can't understand what it would have meant for me to refuse. It would have been a betrayal.'

'You disgust me.' She burst into tears, brushing his arms away as he reached out to comfort her. She walked slowly around the room sobbing, shaking her head slowly, her hands covering her face.

He reached for his diary to check the number and then dialled. As always, the girl answered.

'Can I help you?'

'I want to speak to Mr Paynter.'

'I'm afraid he's not available at the moment.'

'When is he available?'

'Maybe I can help you. What is it about?'

'I want you to get a message to Mr Paynter. Tell him I must speak to him urgently. It's a matter of life and death. You understand?'

'And your name, sir?'

'Said. Khalim Said.'

'I'll pass on your message, sir.'

In London Paynter put down the parallel receiver.

'Well done.' He grinned. 'I was right. You could hear the panic in his voice. The bastards don't like it when they're on the receiving end themselves.' He looked at his watch. 'Let him sweat for half an hour and we'll call him back. Should just catch the highlights of the Test Match. Give me a shout in my office when it's time.'

'Right, sir.'

Paynter dialled the number and smiled as the receiver at the other end was picked up on the first ring.

'Mr Khalim?'

'Yes.'

'Paynter here. You called me.'

'I want my children, Paynter. I want them back in twenty-four hours.'

'I don't understand. Why phone me about your children?'

'They've been taken, Paynter. Kidnapped.'

'That must be very disturbing. How can I help you?'

'It's your people, you bastard. They want me to free Mason in exchange for my children.'

'I see.' He waited. 'Seems a very sensible idea to me. Are you making the necessary arrangements?'

'It's not in my control, Paynter. You know that. I was just an intermediary.'

'Not quite, Mr Khalim,' Paynter said softly, 'You played your part.'

'I only passed messages back and forth. Nothing more.'

'I was thinking of Mason's wife, Mr Said. The girl in Paris. Remember?'

There were several moments of silence and then the Arab said, 'Are you going to help, Paynter? Or do I go to the police?'

'You'd have a lot to explain to the Dutch police, Mr Said. Abuse of your diplomatic status, involvement in kidnapping an Englishman, attempting to blackmail the British government. The world press would have a wonderful time . . . and you would still have the problem of your children.' He paused. 'Why don't you have a word with your friends in Damascus? I understand they've got what they wanted. The equipment is working. They will want to keep their side of the bargain, I'm sure. You said several times that they could be trusted. Men of honour, you said. Remember? I have tapes of all our conversations if you need reminding.'

'What do you want me to do, you bastard?'

'Come, come, Mr Said. Vulgarity won't get us anywhere. It sounds as if it would be wise to go along with what these people say, or they might feel that what was good enough for Mason was good enough for your children.'

'What does that mean?'

'You suggested that your friends might get impatient and kill poor Mason. The people who hold your children might be equally impatient.'

'You mean you would kill my children in cold blood?'

'I resent that comment, Mr Said. I resent it very much. You asked for advice and I gave it. Your problem has nothing to do with me. You have involved yourself in a very dangerous situation. I assume you did that voluntarily. It hasn't worked out as you expected and it's up to you to solve the problem. Not me.'

'Damascus might not do as I ask.'

'I'm sure they will, Mr Said. At least you should try. And quickly too.'

'If I can arrange this, you will cooperate?'

'I'm in no position to cooperate but if the other parties referred to me I should recommend they assist you in any way they could.'

'I curse you, Paynter. In the name of my family, I curse you.'

And Said hung up, aware of his wife standing silently watching him from the doorway. He looked at his watch. It was one o'clock in the morning in Damascus but he reached for the phone.

For half an hour he pleaded and cursed in gutter Arabic, angered by the coolness and calmness of the two men he spoke to.

An hour later as he sat exhausted in the armchair the phone rang and a different voice, a voice with a faint accent said, 'Are you ready to make the exchange, Said?'

His voice was hoarse from shouting as he said, 'For God's sake, I'm not in control of Mason. There are others to persuade.'

'You'd better hurry up, my friend. Your little girl is getting rather upset. We can't wait around much longer. Maybe another twenty-four hours.'

And the line went dead.

Paynter phoned Rennie and gave him a cryptic description of his conversation with Said and no sooner had Rennie hung up than the door-bell rang. It was Ryan, looking worried.

'We've got a problem, Johnny. I'm not sure what to do.'

'Sit down. Whisky or gin?'

'Whisky.'

As Rennie handed him the drink he said, 'What's the problem?'

'It's the girl, Nadia. When she came to, she was obviously in a bit of a state. Trembling and crying. We put Josh on to smoothing her down a bit. He's got five kids of his own and knows how to joke them out of a mood. But she doesn't speak much English. She speaks mainly Dutch and a bit of Italian and Arabic, so he didn't get far.

'She wouldn't eat anything. We put her to bed and tonight she was awake. At least she'd got her eyes open . . . and that's how she's been ever since. She's breathing OK, her temperature's normal but she doesn't speak or move or show any signs of recognition of anybody. We brought her brother in but she didn't respond.'

'What do you think it is?'

'I don't know. It's like she's in coma. I'm not a medic but it looks like some kind of trauma to me.'

'Have you tried sitting her up, moving her around?'

'She's just limp like a rag doll.'

'How's the boy?'

'He's OK. Being very Brit and stiff upper lip. Seeing his sister like that upset him but he tried not to show it.'

'What have you got in mind?'

'Give her another day, maybe two, and if she doesn't improve we'd better fly in one of our own doctors.' He was silent for a moment. 'How much longer is it going to take?'

'It's stuck at the moment. Said's mates in Damascus are the ones who have to break the log-jam. They won't like losing face.'

Ryan stood up. 'I'd better get back. I'll keep in touch if there's any development you need to know. By the way, Paynter said in London that it might be necessary to tape an appeal from his kids to play to him. I've got a Uher if you need it?'

'Forget it, Pat. That's Paynter's thinking, not mine. We haven't sunk that low yet.'

'See you soon.'

'OK.'

Adele Palmer was just opening the gallery when he got there the next morning.

He smiled. 'Any chance of taking you out for a meal today?'

Her face was pale and her eyes red-rimmed and he guessed that Said or Gabriella had told her the news.

She sighed. 'Thanks for the invitation, Johnny. But I'm afraid I'm not in the mood.'

'What's the matter?'

For a moment he thought she was going to tell him and then she said, 'I promised to stay with Gabbie tonight.'

'Let's take them for a meal too.'

Her lips trembled and a tear rolled down one cheek. She could barely speak as she said softly, 'Something dreadful's happened, Johnny. Gabbie's out of her mind.'

'What's happened?'

'I promised not to tell anyone.' She looked towards the window for long moments and then back to his face. 'Would you help them if they asked you to?'

'How can I say, Adele, when I don't know what it's all about?'

'Would you do something for me . . . walk round the block for ten minutes while I phone Gabbie.'

'Sure. Is ten minutes enough?'

'Yes. Ample.'

Rennie walked slowly in the sunshine and after the ten minutes were up he went back to the gallery. Adele Palmer seemed to have recovered her composure.

'I spoke to Khalim and Gabriella. She had suggested they talk to you.' She looked at his face. 'You said you were in Amsterdam to find a missing person. Is that true?'

He nodded. 'Yes.'

'Do you swear that?'

'If you insist. Yes. But why does it matter?'

She took a deep breath and exhaled slowly as if she were building up her courage. 'Gabriella wants to see you. She's coming here in a few minutes. Against Khalim's wishes. He says he will divorce her if she speaks to you about her problem.'

'What's the problem?'

'She wants you to find her children. They've been kidnapped. She will pay you herself. Anything you ask. Will you help her? She's desperate.'

'Let me talk to her first.'

'Please help her, Johnny. I can't bear to see her so distressed.' She looked over his shoulder. 'Here she is. Be kind.'

The pupils of Gabriella's eyes were so dilated that her brown eyes looked almost black. She was wearing a white summer dress. Adele brought a chair over for her to sit on.

'I've told Johnny, Gabbie.'

Rennie said softly, 'Tell me about Khalim. Why did he forbid you to talk to me? Maybe he has a good reason. Maybe he is in control of the situation and an outsider could spoil it.'

'He's not in control. He is helpless. Let me tell you what has happened.'

She told him everything she knew and when she had finished he said, 'Let me go and speak to Khalim. You stay here with Adele.'

Five minutes later he was at Said's apartment. It was a long time after he pressed the bell that the cook answered the door. He nodded to her, ignoring her protests and walked through into the living room. Said was sitting with the telephone on his knees. He shook his head at Rennie.

'I don't want you to help, Mr Rennie.'

'I haven't offered you my help, Khalim. Gabriella has told me what happened. She's with Adele. She asked me to find the children but I said I would want to speak to you first.'

Khalim shrugged exaggeratedly. 'Why pass up a chance of making money?'

'Can we talk?'

'There's no point.'

'Can we talk?'

'I can't stop you.'

'You only have to ask me to leave Khalim, and I'll leave.'

'There is nothing anyone can do. Not me, not you, not anyone else.'

'May I sit down?'

Khalim pointed at a chair and when Rennie was sitting, facing Khalim, he said, 'Do you know where the English-man is being held?'

'Yes. He's on a boat on the Hilversum canal just above a boating lake called Loosdrechtse.'

'Could you take me there if it was necessary?'

'Yes.'

'Could you show me on a map where it is?'

'Yes.'

'How many of your men are at the boat?'

'They're not my men, Rennie. They're . . . not . . . my men.' Khalim was almost screaming.

'How many men, Khalim?'

'So far as I know there are five.'

'All Arabs?'

'No. Only one Arab. He is in charge.'

'Would he obey an order from you?'

'Of course not. He would laugh at me.'

'Who put him in charge?'

'The people in Damascus.'

'What did they say when you spoke to them?'

'They were cool. Said they would consider it and let me know.'

'When will they let you know?'

'God knows. They didn't say.'

'How did you leave it?'

'I cursed them. I swore that if they didn't do it I would never lift a finger again for Palestine or any Arab country.' He shrugged. 'I reacted like a camel-driver not a diplomat.'

'How important are they? How near the top?'

Said shrugged. 'Three steps down. Thereabouts.'

'What other governments are involved? What about the ayatollahs?'

'They know. They supplied most of the funds but they're not involved otherwise.'

'Could you prove that Damascus and Teheran are involved?'

'Not on paper.'

'But you could give details of who approached you?'

'Yes.'

'Gabbie said that the Arab who's got Mason wouldn't carry out their orders. Do the people in Damascus know that?'

'I'm sure they do. But now they don't want to lose face by having their orders refused.'

'This chap in London that Gabbie mentioned, Paynter. Have you got a number where you can call him?'

'Yes.'

'Do you want me to help you?'

'How can you, Johnny? Nobody can help me.'

Rennie saw that Said was beginning to soften.

'I think I can. In fact I'm sure I can.'

'Why should you get involved?'

'Do you want me to help or don't you? I'm used to

dealing with this sort of situation. I could have your kids back in a couple of days.'

'What could you do?'

'The first thing is for you and Gabriella to move out to a hotel. Somewhere out of the centre. The Amstel would do fine.'

'Why, for God's sake? I've got to be here for the phone.'

'Your friends in Damascus will be getting scared that you might bring in the police or talk to the press. They'd never live it down. They'll want to wipe you out. Both of you.'

Khalim looked aghast. 'They are friends of mine.'

'Why did you get involved with this, Khalim?'

'For the sake of my country, Palestine.'

'And that's the way they'll square their consciences when they have you both killed. It'll all be in a good cause.'

'And if we move out?'

'I'll take over here. I'll negotiate with Paynter.'

'I suppose you're used to this sort of thing because of your job?'

'Yes. And you're emotionally involved. They know that. They know how vulnerable you are.'

'Let me go and talk with Gabbie.'

An hour later Rennie was back at Prinsengracht. Khalim, Gabbie and the servants had moved out to the Amstel Hotel before he left. Said had shown him on an ANWB map where the boat was moored. He dialled his number for Paynter and waited as the lines clicked through. Paynter himself answered.

'Paynter speaking.'

'It's Rennie.'

'Jesus. I've been going crazy trying to contact you. What the hell's going on?'

'Said's officially appointed me to take over the negotiation for him.'

'You're joking.'

'I'm not. He's desperate but his friends in foreign parts aren't in a hurry. Apart from that, their representative here is unlikely to carry out their orders. He's a nutter. He likes what he's doing.'

'How do you know all this, Johnny? And how, why, did you get Said to hand over?'

'I haven't got time to explain. I'm worried that the nutter might blow it all up by finishing off our mutual friend.'

'So who are you going to negotiate with?'

'Nobody.'

There were several seconds' silence and then Paynter said, 'Go on.'

'I'm going to deal with the nutter myself. Soonest.'

'So you know where our friend is then?'

'Within a mile or so. I'll find him OK.'

'I don't like all this, Johnny. It sounds real crazy.'

'It is. But it's the only way.'

'I could try asking the FO to put pressure on Damascus. They'd blow their tops but they might cooperate.'

'It would take too long. And Damascus would just say they didn't know what we were talking about.'

'Well, on your head be it. But for Christ's sake keep it low-key. If it becomes public the balloon will really go up. Understood?'

'Understood.'

Rennie walked back to Said's place intending to see if there was any hard evidence of Said's connection with Mason's kidnapping in case it was ever needed to satisfy a court or an internal enquiry. But a few moments after he arrived the door-bell rang. For a moment he hesitated and then he walked through the short hall passage and opened the front door.

There was a police car outside and two uniformed policemen.

Chapter 19

THE OLDER policeman said, 'Mijnheer Said?'

Rennie shook his head. 'He's not here. Can I help you?'

'Maybe. We'd like to talk with somebody.'

The two policemen followed him into the sitting room, glancing around it before they sat.

'We are from BAR, the Criminal Investigation Section of the Amsterdam police. We're investigating a murder.'

'How can I help?'

'Where is Mr Said?'

'He's away for a few days. I'm not sure where they are. Touring I think. I'm just looking after the flat for them.'

'Where are his children?'

'They are with him so far as I know. But what does all this have to do with a murder?'

'A taxi-driver was attacked and made unconscious with some chemical. He had a weak heart. He never recovered consciousness and he died late last night.'

He waited for Rennie to comment but when he sat silent the policeman went on. 'We checked with the company who employ him and it seems he had a regular trip every day to take the Said children to school. We know from his girlfriend that he intended to pick them up as usual the morning he was attacked.'

'When was this?'

'Three days ago.'

'The Said children haven't been to school all this week.'

'We know that. We checked at the school. May I ask your name?'

'Rennie. John Rennie.'

'Are you English?'

'Yes.'

'What are you doing here in Amsterdam?'

'I'm here on business. I'm employed by a large firm of solicitors in London.'

'We found children's fingerprints in the taxi. We'd like to compare them with the Said children's prints. When will they be back?'

'They said five or six days.'

'Will you be in contact with Mr Said?'

'He said he would phone to say when they are on their way back.'

'Perhaps you would ask him to contact us as soon as possible.'

Both policemen stood up. The older man said, 'Did Mr Said seem worried when you last saw him?'

'I wouldn't say that. Why should he be worried?'

'There was a theory we had. It doesn't seem likely but it would fit what we know.'

'What was the theory?'

The policeman smiled. 'Policemen's theories should never be for publication. Thank you for your help.'

Again they looked casually but intently around the room as they left. After Rennie let them out it was almost ten minutes before he heard their car start up. He abandoned the search and headed back to Prinsengracht.

Back at his own flat he gathered together things he needed – binoculars, maps, the portable transceiver – and then took the parts of the pistol from the inside of the lead-lined, spare radio-case. He assembled it slowly and carefully. He had only twenty rounds in the two magazines. But if they weren't enough then it would no longer be his problem. He cut sandwiches and wrapped them in a damp cloth and ate two boiled eggs as he looked at the large-scale map. It would be quicker to drive down the A2 and turn off east onto the road to the big Loosdrechtse lake and then go up towards the windmill. But that's the way they would expect anyone to come. If he took the road to Weesp and then south to Nederhorst he would go through the town and leave the car well before the windmill.

He slept soundly for four hours and then washed and

shaved slowly and carefully. The car-hire offices were only just opening when he arrived. He filled in the form, showed them his passport and paid the deposit.

He stopped in the suburbs and bought a butcher's knife, some wide medical adhesive plaster and two short lengths of nylon boat rope. He also bought a thermos and had it filled with coffee at a restaurant, and his last purchases were a kilo of pears and some bread, and a copy of that day's *De Telegraaf*. There was a paragraph about a dead taxi-driver but so far as he could make out there was no suggestion that it was murder.

As he got to Weesp itself he saw a man on a cycle with fishing-rods tied to the crossbar and the wicker basket on the carrier at the back. He walked the streets for ten minutes before he found it. It was a hardware shop that had fishing rods in a case by the door. He had never fished in his life but the owner of the shop showed him what to buy and how to assemble the rod with its line, hook and old-fashioned centre-pin reel. He bought a keep-net, a small folding canvas stool and a tin of worms.

He parked the car just under a kilometre from the windmill. There was a sign that pointed to the next village – Vreeland.

The sky was blue but there was a breeze disturbing the water of the canal, bending the reeds and grass as he walked along the bank. There was a sort of embankment that rose up five or six feet before sloping down to the fields on the other side. The slopes were covered with a mass of field poppies and clumps of white marguerites.

Kneeling at the top of the embankment he focused the binoculars on the centre boat of the three. As Jan had said it was big and ugly, designed to draw coal-barges, not as a pleasure boat. It was about fifty feet long, very wide, and low in the water with a wooden wheelhouse at the far end with flaking white paint. In front of the wheelhouse was a crude ventilator stack. He could just make out the painted name on the bow – *Het Vlaamsche Leeuw – The Flemish Lion*. There was a man sitting on a wooden chair outside the wheelhouse; Rennie watched as he lit a cigarette. The nearest boat was a GRP launch about 27 feet long and the canvas covers were all tied down. The furthest boat was only just visible, almost two hundred metres from the gang's boat.

Rennie went down the embankment into the field and walked along about three hundred metres. Crawling up the embankment he lay prone at the top, pulling out the lens hoods of the binoculars to cut off any reflection before he peered out through the tall green stalks of cow-parsley that fringed the top of the bank.

There were two men visible now on the boat. The man who was smoking had his head back against the wheelhouse and his eyes were closed, and Rennie guessed that it wasn't just tobacco that he was smoking. His skin was a light brown and he had a pock-marked clean-shaven face. The man standing in front of him was obviously the Arab. He wore just a towel around his waist. His hair was black and he had a moustache and beard and his lean smooth body was much darker. He was standing with his hands on his hips and Rennie could faintly hear his angry voice as he shouted at the man who was smoking.

There was no sign of the other men for almost an hour, then one of them came into sight from the direction of the windmill and as Rennie refocused he saw that it was two men, one on a cycle and the other walking alongside.

Rennie realised that they must be very confident that they had not been traced. It was all very casual and undisciplined. His mind went back to those early days of training. Have a clear plan of what you intend to do. Then do it. It was a dictum he believed in. Some people liked complex plans with variations for all eventualities. People always remarked on how easily he carried out his missions. Experience had told him that it always was easy provided your intention was clear. If it wasn't easy it seldom worked. And if it did there were more casualties than there need be.

He had only one objective. To kill the Arab. He was the key. When the others saw him die it would be enough. They were thugs but they were neither fanatics nor psychopaths. It wasn't their cause. They were just hired hands. Unreliable hands from the look of them.

The two men went on board with a cardboard box that

looked as if it held groceries, leaving the cycle lying on the grass of the embankment.

Somebody drew back one of the curtains on the portholes but Rennie could see nothing inside. A radio was switched on and he could hear the drone of an announcement and then music, rock or reggae, he didn't know which.

He made his way back along the field almost up to the lock gates. There was only one thing he wanted to know now and that was the layout of the wheelhouse and the way down to the interior of the boat.

Sitting on the canal bank he assembled the rod and the line and the reel, sticking the point of the hook into the cork handle as the man in the shop had shown him. With his haversack over one shoulder and the rod over the other he started the walk back towards the boats.

As he approached the boats he stopped every few yards and looked at the water as if he were judging his chances of a fish. As he walked alongside the boat the Arab was sitting on a box on the small aft deck. Rennie nodded to him as he passed but the Arab ignored him as he carried on wiping his neck with a cloth. There were no doors on the wheelhouse and there were double swing doors leading down below decks.

He settled down on the side of the canal just ahead of the third boat, two hundred yards away from *The Flemish Lion*. Slowly and carefully he baited the hook, cast the float a few feet into the canal and settled down on the small canvas seat.

At midday he ate the sandwiches and poured a drink from the thermos into its plastic cap. Just once he heard a shout from the boat but otherwise there was silence. A few passing barges created a gentle wash that sent a small wave through the reeds at the edge of the canal. As the heat shimmered on the water he moved to the shade of the embankment lying back as if he were sleeping. From the extra height he could see the whole of the after-deck and the wheelhouse. There was one man, asleep, sitting on a coil of rope, leaning back against the rails on the far side. He counted twelve slats on the boarding plank and the distance to the steps leading below deck was about seven feet.

As the sun began to set he gathered together his things and walked back along the towpath. The Arab was just coming up from below decks and he stopped for a moment, glancing at Rennie, as he shook the sleeping man awake.

Rennie passed by without turning his head and when he next looked back the boats were invisible in the evening mist that rose from the canal.

He turned the car by the old lock-gates and backed it slowly down the towpath for about fifty yards so that it was a little nearer the boat and facing the right way for when he wanted to leave.

He wrapped the nylon rope around his waist and tied it loosely and took only the knife and the gun and the roll of adhesive plaster as he walked back down the canal.

When he saw the lights from the wheelhouse he went up over the embankment into the fields. Ten minutes later he crawled slowly to the top of the embankment and he was where he expected to be. Right opposite the boat. He looked at his watch in the darkness and pressed the small button that illuminated the dial. It was 9.15. Over three hours before he intended to make a move.

Rennie lay on his back looking up at the stars. It would have been so much easier to have done this right at the start, once Jan had said where he could find the boat. Just knock off the Arab, take Mason, and the party would have been over. Except that those high-born goons in Damascus didn't know then that they'd got a mutineer on the good ship *Flemish Lion*. And nobody could guess how they would have reacted when their sacrificial goat had been released. Who could know what Mason had written and whether or not they had it to use on the media to square the account? If they couldn't come out winners they could make sure that the Brits were losers too. It was one of those doomed operations where all you could do was count the cards as they fell, and hope that you could take a trick with a ten and a jack when it was getting towards the end of the game. But it was what they wanted. Paynter and the high-ups. It wasn't their fault that it had been such a shambles. If

148

the Arabs hadn't got Mason they'd have got somebody else. But it was good thinking to have picked on Mason. A man who'd taken a beating because he'd married the wrong kind of girl. Somebody else might have taken his pill rather than talk.

And Khalim Said. He might be a good diplomat and even a good businessman but it was fatal for a man to walk away from his own character. When they had conned Khalim Said into seducing Fleur Mason as proof of his patriotism he may well have thought of Jerusalem and Palestine while he was performing but it had involved him up to his neck. He'd probably expected that that was the big sacrifice and would be the end of the matter. And when they insisted that he become the go-between he wouldn't have needed to be told of the subtle hold they now had on him. A word from some anonymous voice from Damascus in Gabriella's ear would have been enough to tear them apart. Khalim Said wasn't cut out for the realities of what went on under all the diplomatic hypocrisy. He could probably fine-tune some diplomatic manoeuvring but when it came down to the real world he was a lamb sent to the slaughter.

Despite the day's sun it was beginning to turn cold. He would have been glad of a drink from the Thermos but it would have got in the way. The rope, the plaster, the gun and the knife were the essentials. And it was a time for essentials.

Moving back to the crest of the embankment he peered towards the boat. There was a figure in the shadows where the gangplank rested on the canal bank. Whoever it was was smoking and he coughed before shuffling back up the gangplank to the after-deck. It was the Arab, and Rennie watched as the man walked across to the far rails and spat into the canal.

For a moment Rennie hesitated, then he drew back the slide on the pistol, tightened the silencer and slipped up the safety catch. Some ducks fluttered and quacked on the far side of the canal as Rennie went on all fours down the embankment, moving silently to the shadow where the Arab had been standing a few minutes before. There was the sweet smell of dope in the air. He backed off a little so that he could see the deck. The man was still leaning over the rails and Rennie slid the pistol back into his side-pocket and took the knife from his inside jacket pocket. He eased off his shoes and crouched as he went up the gangplank and across the deck. The Arab didn't turn until he was three feet away: he saw the knife in Rennie's hand and as he opened his mouth to shout Rennie's left hand smashed sideways against his wind-pipe and his right hand rammed the knife into the man's bare chest. He felt it jar and turn against a rib but it went on its way right up to the handle until he felt the gush of warm blood over the back of his hand. He lowered the Arab to the deck and cursed himself for not bringing a torch.

Halfway down the companion-way he pushed open the double doors and kept them open with his shoulders. The stench of humanity and dope fumes was nauseating. With one hand he felt around for a light switch and couldn't find one. His hand closed over the butt of the pistol in his pocket and, taking it out, he fired one shot into the darkness. The crack echoed round for long seconds and then a light came on. It was one of the Surinamese, naked, peering across the saloon from the corridor that seemed to lead to the cabins.

He beckoned the man forward. He was way out high, stumbling his uncertain way across the saloon. He was panting, his eyes rolling as Rennie said, 'Waar is Engelsman?'

The man pointed to the far end of the passageway. Rennie turned him and prodded him with the gun, pushing the man ahead of him. A cabin door opened and a brown face looked out. Rennie slammed the cabin door against the face and the man screamed with pain.

Mason was lying on filthy blankets on the bunk. A light was on, the switch taped over. He looked terrible. 'What's going on?' he whispered.

'It's Rennie, Mason, John Rennie. Take my gun and get off the boat and wait for me.'

Mason staggered as he tried to get to his feet and Rennie took his arm and pushed him towards the passageway. Rennie kept the gun. Mason couldn't have held it, let alone fired it.

150

There were seven cabins and only three were occupied. One with the man nursing the smashed nose, rocking slowly on his bunk. In the other two the men were out cold. When Rennie looked around he saw the stubby pipes and little brown pellets in saucers.

He locked the half-mobile Surinamese in one of the cabins and headed for the wheelhouse. Mason was lying on the embankment. There was no point in tying up the men, they wouldn't be active for hours and even then they wouldn't have recovered enough to do anything.

Mason cowered back as Rennie stood over him and Rennie realised that Mason wasn't going to be able to walk. It was almost a mile to the car.

Rennie knelt beside him, and Mason turned his face away. He struggled a little as Rennie lifted him onto his shoulder and stood up. Mason was sickeningly light. Rennie hurried as fast as he could along the towpath in case someone had heard the shot and reported it.

Twice he had to stop and lower Mason to the grassy embankment and the second time Mason vomited.

He laid Mason on the back seat of the car and then walked round to the boot and unlocked it. He took out the portable transceiver, switched on and pressed the call button. There was no response and Rennie looked at his watch. It was 1.15 a.m. On the third attempt there was a reply and a voice said, 'Pyramid.'

Rennie said, 'Is "R" there? This is Sandwich calling. It's urgent.'

'Hold on. He'll call you back.'

Rennie switched off the acoustic indicator and turned the pointer to 'Visual' and less than a minute later the red light was blinking and the LED showed 'SPK'.

'Sandwich speaking. Can you hear me?'

'Loud and clear.'

'The two pixies to go to their home address for ten hundred hours. Understood?'

'Understood. Will deliver. Quack advisable, situation deteriorating.'

'Maybe I'll be there. Don't recognise me. Out.'

'Roger.'

The journey back to Amsterdam seemed interminable. But the roads were almost free of any other traffic. Just a few lorries heading for the markets.

He parked the car a hundred yards from his apartment. The Prinsengracht was empty, but as the army always said, 'Time spent in reconnaissance is seldom wasted.'

Inside the apartment everything was exactly as he had left it.

Mason was conscious and Rennie drove the car right up to the open door of the apartment and carried him inside. He put him gently onto the big soft sofa. Rennie carefully undressed him and bathed his face and body. There were welts across his ribs and belly and his scrotum looked like a raw red balloon. When he had carried Mason to one of the beds he looked at his watch. He would phone Said at 6.30. Meanwhile he would report to London and then have a bath.

The duty officer took his call. They would contact Paynter immediately. He had given orders to be woken whenever Rennie called. He could expect a return call inside fifteen minutes. Five minutes later the phone rang.

'Is that you, Johnny'

'Yes. It's done. Mason's with me. We'll be returning our small friends to their owners this morning.'

'That's bloody marvellous, Johnny. Congratulations. First class. Was it difficult?'

'No. If it had been difficult it wouldn't have worked.'

'My God, I'm relieved. It's been hanging over everything like a big black cloud. When will you be back'

'Do you want me to debrief Mason while he's here'

'Might be easier. More likely to talk now than later. No time to concoct some cock and bull story. How is he?'

'In pretty bad shape but he'll be OK in a few days.'

'Well, again, congratulations. It won't be forgotten, I assure you. Bloody marvellous.'

'OK. See you.'

'Take care.'

Rennie hung up and closed his eyes, putting his hands up to his face, rubbing it slowly to relax the muscles.

When he had bathed and shaved he went in to look at

Mason. Rennie had little sympathy for agents who succumbed to pressure and talked when they were caught. There was always the option of that small yellow pill and oblivion. Not even the old agony of prussic acid, but a painless micro-second to nothingness. But Mason's body had been systematically abused. The work of a sadist not an opponent seeking information. His mouth gaped open, his breathing stertorous. But given a few days he would be fit to send to London if somebody went with him. If he could sleep for twenty-four hours he would be fit enough to talk.

At 6.30 a.m. he phoned the Amstel and the porter put him through to the Saids' suite. Said's voice was a monotone.

'Khalim Said.'

'Said, this is John Rennie. The children will be back at your place at ten o'clock. I suggest you and Gabriella go over as soon as it's convenient.'

There was a long silence. 'You mean that? It's not just a hope?'

'No. They'll be there at ten.'

Rennie heard Said say something in Arabic and it sounded like some sort of prayer. Then Said said quietly, 'I can't believe it, Johnny. How did you do it? Can I wake Gabbie and tell her?'

'Of course you can. I'll go over and wait for you both.'

Rennie let himself into the Saids' apartment and twenty minutes later they arrived with the servants. Khalim Said hugged him, smiling and excited. Gabriella still looked pale and stunned. Not quite believing, and not quite back out of her nightmare. She walked aimlessly from room to room. Touching things, adjusting a cushion, moving an ornament, then standing, sighing, arms folded across her chest, looking towards the windows but seeing nothing.

A little later Said took Rennie into his small study.

'Tell me how you did it, Johnny?'

'Just forget it, Khalim. Just be glad that they're back.'

'Did you have to pay a ransom?'

'No. Just forget it. The Englishman has been handed

over to his friends and that's the end of it all.'

'But how can I repay you, Johnny?'

'Just do what I say. Forget it. All of it.' Rennie told him about the police and their questions about the children, and told Said to stick to the same story. The kids were with them on tour. He went on, 'I'm going back to my place now.'

'Whatever you say, Johnny.'

'Can I give you some advice?'

'Of course.'

'Don't talk to the children about what happened until they've settled back in their usual routine. If they want to talk let them talk but don't ask them questions.'

'I'll do just what you say, and Johnny, how can I thank you for what you've done?'

'Like I told you, Khalim. Just forget it.'

Rennie slept for six hours and then tried to contact Ryan on the portable. There was no response, not even the hum of a carrier wave. They were probably already on their way to Schiphol, maybe even back in London.

He drove the car round to the Saids' apartment. Said himself let him in. The elation had gone and he looked distraught. 'What's the matter, Khalim?'

'It's Nadia. She just doesn't speak. She just sits there and looks at us. Gabbie's right at the end of her tether. I just don't know what to do.'

For a few moments Rennie stood with his eyes closed, thinking. When he opened them he said, 'Have you got a flat or a house in any other country, Khalim?'

'Yes. I've got a house just outside Los Angeles, a flat in Geneva and a house in Amman.'

Rennie nodded. 'I think you all need a change of scene. You need medical advice. Whatever doctor you use you'll need to tell him as much as he needs to know about what's happened. If you use a Dutch doctor he's going to feel a conflict of interest between his discretion to you and his patriotic duty. It would only need a hint to the authorities and the whole thing could blow up. I suggest you go to your place in California and find a good physician there.'

'We can't go on like this, Johnny. I thought it would be a day of celebration but it's been dreadful. Not just little Nadia, but Gabbie too. I can't take any more.'

'What do you want to do? Would you like me to fix your flight arrangements for you?'

Said closed his eyes, slowly shaking his head. 'How soon can you get us away?'

'Where to?'

'To the States.'

'Let me come up and use your phone. You put Gabbie in the picture. How long do you need to get ready?'

'We can leave in half an hour. We have all we need in the other house.'

Rennie looked at his watch as he dialled the airport. It was 8.20. There was a KLM flight to New York via Shannon at midnight and Rennie used Said's American Express card to book their places.

He arranged for a taxi to pick the Saids up at ten and walked over to where Gabbie was sitting alone on the couch. She was shivering violently as if she had an ague and as he bent down to speak to her she waved him away.

Khalim was talking to the servants and Rennie said, 'The tickets are at the KLM desk at Schiphol. I hope things improve out there.'

Rennie held out his hand and Said took it in both of his. There were tears in his eyes. He shrugged hopelessly. 'Thanks, Johnny. Thanks for everything.'

Rennie smiled and said softly, *'Salaam alyekum.'*

Chapter 20

HE MADE Mason sip slowly at a cup of warm broth from a can. It would be a couple of days before he'd start talking to him about what had happened. When Mason was in bed Rennie phoned London and Paynter got him transferred to the medical section. He described Mason's condition as best he could and they told him how to treat his wounds and the sort of diet he would need.

It was three days before Mason was fit to talk of his experiences and it was obvious that there were periods that he couldn't remember at all. The one bright spot was Mason's insistence that all the names and dates and operations that he'd written down had been entirely fictitious. They had no way of checking on anything and he had realised that. What he had written would have been useless to them. The only hard information he had given them was Paynter's name and telephone number. Rennie went over this point with Mason again and again. In the end he believed him. Mason was basically fit now and the improvement in his physical condition was noticeable. It was Mason himself who broached the subject of his return to London.

'What do they intend to do when I get back to London, Johnny?'

'I guess they'll give you at least a couple of weeks' leave.'

'I mean after that. Will they chuck me out?'

'There's been no hint of that.'

'They won't like it that I gave them Paynter's identity and telephone number.'

'Maybe not but there were mitigating circumstances.'

'How d'you mean?'

Rennie sighed. 'You were at a low ebb when they got

you. Your private problems.'

'Does she know what happened to me?'

'No. She doesn't even know you went missing. She just knew I was trying to contact you.'

'Do you think she'd be sympathetic if she knew what they'd done to me?'

Rennie sighed. 'Yes. I'm sure she would be. But not in the way you want. She said nothing unpleasant about you but you've got to get used to the fact that it's over.' He looked at Mason and said quietly, 'She's burned her bridges and yours. There's no going back.'

'You mean the other men?'

'Not just that. She closed her mind to any reconciliation way back. She signalled that when she moved back to Paris. She was closing the door on London, and you.'

'I still love her.'

'Look, Harry. Forget her. It's over. And you'd never have succeeded anyway. Not even if you'd given up your job. There would have been some other excuse.'

'You didn't like her then?'

'No I didn't. She's very pretty but she's French and selfish. And she's far tougher than you are. And she's a woman. If they let you down once they'll do it again, no matter what they say.'

'You're a hard nut, Johnny, aren't you?'

'I know what will work and what won't. I don't kid myself. I face the facts and you should do the same. There's plenty of pretty girls who are far more suitable for you than that one. You'll look back on all this one day when you're happily married and you'll thank God that you escaped.'

Mason half-smiled, his lip trembling. 'Find me one, Johnny.'

'It's time you were in bed. I'm going round to see a friend of mine. Don't answer the door-bell or the phone. I'll be back in about an hour.'

The lights were on in Adele Palmer's flat and he rang the bell and waited. She was in her dressing-gown when she opened the door.

'Am I disturbing you?'

She shook her head. 'No. Come in and have a drink.' She sighed as he followed her up the stairs. 'I could do with some company.'

Without asking she poured them both a whisky and sat down facing him. 'Khalim phoned me this morning.'

'How are things with them?'

'You haven't heard?'

'No.'

'Little Nadia's in some sort of mental home. From what I can gather she's no more than a zombie now. They found an Italian-speaking psychiatrist. Gabbie thinks he's good but Nadia doesn't recognise Khalim or Gabriella. The medics are bandying around words like "catatonic state". And Gabbie blames it all on Khalim. She's asked him to move out. Says the marriage is over.'

'How's he taking it?'

'It's the last straw for him. He's right at the end of his tether.'

'Did you visit them when they were at the hotel?'

'Only once. That was enough. It was obvious that there was nothing I could do to improve things. She seemed to blame Khalim for everything that had happened.' She paused. 'You know, I used to see them as the perfect couple. Lively, intelligent, gentle and loving. I'd have bet my last guilder on them never breaking up. And now. In ten days it's as good as finished. How the hell can that happen, Johnny? Was it Khalim's fault?'

It was a long time before Rennie answered and then he said quietly, 'I guess indirectly it was. Would you like to go out for a meal?'

She smiled. 'Thanks, but no. All this depresses me terribly.'

'Don't think about it. If you want to help when the time's ripe you'll need to be calm and bright. Your usual self. Stay on dry land. If you get in the quagmire with them you won't be able to help them out. You'll sink with them.'

She smiled. 'How about I do us a fry-up?'

Rennie smiled back. 'I'd enjoy that.'

Rennie sent his notes on the debriefing of Mason back to Paynter through Lambert at the consulate and the diplomatic bag.

The following day he walked across to the room in Warmoesstraat. He half expected that she would have left already but she was there, and she was obviously delighted to see him.

'I thought you must have gone back to England already. Tea, coffee or hot chocolate?'

He smiled. 'Hot chocolate if you've got it.'

She looked at his face. 'Has anything happened?'

'Why do you ask that?'

'I'm not sure. I think it's your eyes. They generally look all shiny and alive. They look a bit sad. In fact your whole face looks sad. What is it?'

'Nothing that you and a mug of hot chocolate won't cure.'

She said over her shoulder from the sink, 'I heard from my father a couple of days ago. Said to give you his good wishes if you were still around.'

'That's nice of him. What have *you* been doing?'

'Thinking mainly. Like you said I should.'

She put the two mugs of hot chocolate on the table and sat down facing him, smiling with pleasure as she looked at him.

'It's great to see you again. What have *you* been doing? Or shouldn't I ask?'

He smiled. 'Tell me what you've been thinking about?'

'I thought about you as well as me.'

'How did I make out?'

She laughed. 'You came out of it fine. You always do. Not on all counts but on most.'

'Tell me more.'

'Which bits do you want to hear?'

'The failings. The minus factors.'

She wrinkled her nose. 'They're not exactly failings. More like things that don't fit.'

'So tell me.'

'Part of you really scares me. Sometimes your eyes look like spaniel's eyes but sometimes they're so hard they send shivers down my spine. The way you dealt with that crummy drug-pusher that night. Not just throwing him out but sticking that syringe in his backside. All the way in. My God that must have really hurt him. That's one side. The other's you with me. You pick me up from the gutter, literally the gutter. You give me a bed and food. You don't try to get me into bed. I thought at first you might be a queer.' She laughed softly. 'But by the second day I'd given up that theory.

'I must be a prime example of everything you despise. A squatter, a feckless girl, into the drug scene. Agin authority, spouting my half-baked ideas on how the world should be run. And you actually listened. And discussed it. God knows why you bothered. I must have been a real pain in the neck.' She paused and said softly, 'And yet in your "macho" sort of way you're really quite kind and gentle.

'It's an impossible combination but that's how it is. And I like it.'

'How are you going to put me right?'

She laughed. 'Now you're being sarcastic and that's not fair.'

'I'm not. I want to know. Seriously.'

'What do you do, Johnny? How do you earn your living?'

He shook his head. 'I plead the Fifth and the Fourteenth.'

'OK. You're not going to tell me. But I think that whatever you do you're being wasted.'

'I'll tell my bosses what you think.'

'I can't imagine you having a boss.'

'Why not?'

'I can't imagine you doing anything you don't want to do.'

'Like what?'

She shrugged. 'Something dishonest. Something that's not right. Something you don't like doing.'

'And how did *you* come out of all the thinking?'

She grinned. 'I decided that my ideas were right. But my arguments are no good. What I think is just instinct. I need to justify it better.'

'How are you going to do that?'

'I bought a pile of paperbacks from the American Discount Book Store. Books on politics and economics and social sciences.'

'I'd better start sharpening up my arguments. When are you going back home?'

'I decided in the end not to go home until Christmas but that depends on you.'

'Go on.'

'Can I use this room as long as that?'

'The rent's paid to next June. You can stay as long as you want.'

As he stood up she said softly, 'When shall I see you again?'

'Maybe tomorrow or the day after.'

Rennie checked that Mason was sleeping, poured himself a whisky and settled down in the armchair, his long legs stretched out, his head resting on the back of the chair.

As he had crossed back over the bridge to the Damrak he knew he wanted to get away from Amsterdam. Right now. Mason was fit enough to travel and the operation was over. There was no reason to stay any longer. But as he sat there in the comfortable chair he knew that there were other reasons why he had to go. He wanted to get away from Adele Palmer and Joanna de Vries. Not because he didn't enjoy their company but because of what they said. He needed to get back into his world. A man's world, where he knew the rules and customs, and where self-analysis was only for the weak. He didn't want to spend another minute with people who trusted him.

For the first time in his life John Hamish Rennie was at odds with himself. And it was the outsiders who had caused it. Why the hell should they saddle him with virtues he didn't possess? Virtues that he admired. Honesty, truthfulness and all the rest of it. And his little sermons to Said and the two women. They were what they needed to be told but he wasn't the one who should be telling them. But why not? And Rennie already knew the answer to that question and didn't like it. He found it disturbing.

162

In the last two weeks he had got back Mason, but that was his job. And as part of his job he had killed a man and brought the Said family to the verge of ruin. A broken marriage and a demented girl in a mental institution. He had lied glibly and half-lied without hesitating, and had been praised and thanked by one and all. By Paynter, by the two girls, and Said himself. There was something wrong when your victims thanked you for what you had done to them.

But it was part of the game. It was what he had been trained for. It was what he was good at. So what was wrong with that? What was wrong was that the outsiders should see him as a knight in shining armour, and despite all his rationalising what they saw was what he wanted to be. And what, in his private life, he was. In all his time with SIS he had been secure in the knowledge that what he did was not only in a good cause but was right in itself. If there was violence then it was against people of violence. But was Said a man of violence? Were two small children part of violence? Could you still be called honest if the honesty was only in your personal life? Did the end really justify the means? John Rennie was disturbed and depressed by the thoughts of what he had become. He wasn't sure what he was going to do about it, but instinct told him that something had to be done.

Early the next morning he wrote a letter to Jan Branders explaining that the girl would be using the room in War-moesstraat until the end of December. He thanked Jan for his help and enclosed five thousand guilders. He found a free taxi by the Westerkerk and gave the driver ten guilders to deliver the letter. The man raised his eyebrows when he saw the name and address but nodded and said it would be there in ten minutes.

Rennie booked them on the British Caledonian after-noon flight and started packing his gear. They were over Gatwick just before 5 p.m.

As the landing gear thudded down it was as if they were putting the final full stop at the end of the Amsterdam story. He had been in two minds about saying goodbye to Adele and Joanna and in the end he had decided against it. He wasn't sure why.

Chapter 21

PAYNTER MET them in at Gatwick himself and a pool car drove them all to the Hilton where they had been booked in for the night.

Mason was obviously ill at ease with Paynter and he went straight to his room for the night. Paynter went up with Rennie to his room.

Paynter opened the small room-bar and poured them each a drink. As he looked across at Rennie he lifted his glass.

'Cheers, Johnny. Good to see you back.'

'Cheers.'

'You look pretty knackered. How d'you feel?'

'Tired. A bit out of rhythm.'

Paynter nodded and stood up, putting his empty glass on top of the TV. Rennie said, 'You got my report about the Said family?'

Paynter hunched his shoulders. 'Serve the bugger right. He was bloody well asking for it and he got it. Where the chicken got the chopper. In the neck.' He walked to the door and opened it, pausing. 'Don't bother to come in tomorrow. When are you moving back to your place?'

'Tomorrow.'

'I'll contact you there. We'll have a meeting with Fredericks the next day. You've met Fredericks haven't you?'

'He's the FO liaison chap, isn't he?'

'Yes. Very influential. And a good brain.' He smiled. 'He was holding his breath a bit while you were in Amsterdam.'

'So was I.'

Paynter laughed. 'See you in a couple of days.'

It felt strange when he opened the door of his flat. It was warm and smelled of dust and on the sink there was still the cup and saucer that he had left drying there.

Slowly, as if it was some kind of therapy, he unpacked his bags. Putting things back where they belonged, pushing clothes for washing into the plastic basket and laying out the equipment he had to return to HQ on the dining table.

It looked strange now. Just metal boxes with knobs and switches and dials. Inert and lifeless, clinical and innocent.

He spent an hour in the supermarket and cleaned out his refrigerator beforé packing it with new supplies. He was cleaning out the cupboards when Paynter rang to give him the time and room number of the next day's meeting.

As he vacuumed the carpets in the rooms he knew very well what he was doing. All the cleaning was to give him time to think. Something that he could do without concentrating while he tried to clear his mind.

By mid-evening he had sorted out his priorities. He came to the harsh conclusion that he had been just as weak as Khalim Said. He had gone along with thinking that he didn't agree with. He had crossed the invisible line that marked the difference between loyalty and subservience. Maybe not subservience exactly, but somewhere near it. Paynter and the others were entitled to decide what the ends should be but it had always been up to him to decide the means.

When he had sat in the park that day with Paynter he had known beforehand what was going to be suggested. He had put up a couple of hurdles for Paynter to jump and he'd jumped them effortlessly. And from then on he was in the business of kidnapping children. He hadn't joined SIS to do that. And when he had gone along with it it was the equivalent of Khalim Said's seduction of Mason's wife. Bad thinking. Bad morality. And what was worse was that it hadn't been necessary. He could have gone in and got Mason without the kidnapping. But Paynter wanted the easy way. Just in case it worked.

But there was no need to make a song and dance of it. All he had to do was to mark his distance from such things. Formally and irrevocably so that they would know where he stood. Loyal still, patriotic still, but his own man. And now, when they were all full of congratulations, was the time to clear the air. They would probably share his views. At worst they'd know where he stood.

He was relieved once he had made the decision but still uneasy about what had triggered it. Why should it have taken the naive words of a dropout girl to focus his mind? Why should he have given a second thought to what she said? But he remembered the blue eyes and the look on her face as she listed his virtues in ignorance of the realities of his character. He had known in those moments that if one of them wasn't facing real life it was him not her. Out of the mouths of babes and dropouts.

Rennie wondered why the meeting was to be at the Foreign Office and when he was shown up to Fredericks's office he knew it was more than a routine debriefing meeting. The messenger knocked and a voice called out for them to go in. The man opened the door and said, 'Mr Rennie, sir.'

Fredericks was sitting at his desk and Paynter was standing by the window, looking out towards the river. Fredericks pointed to one of the chairs by the desk. 'Do sit down, Rennie,' he said quietly.

Paynter nodded to Rennie as he walked over slowly and took the other chair.

'I wanted Mr Fredericks to hear from you directly how it went.'

Rennie took a deep breath. 'Before I do that I'd like to make a statement.' And Rennie realised that his voice was louder and harsher than he had meant it to be.

Paynter looked up quickly. 'About what?'

'About the operation.'

Paynter frowned. 'Is this really necessary, Rennie? This is only an informal debriefing.'

'Whatever it is I'd like to make my statement.'

Paynter waved his hand languidly. 'By all means. But don't be too long. We're all busy people as you well know.'

'Right. I'll make it brief. I want to dissociate myself from this operation.'

'*This* operation. It's all over now surely.' Paynter said curtly.

'Not for me it isn't. I'm talking of a matter of principle.'

Paynter smiled. 'Ah . . . principles. That word always worries me. What was it somebody said – "It's easier to create principles than live up to them." I think it was Adlai Stevenson. Anyway . . .' He waved his hand again. '. . . do carry on.'

'I've made my statement. I've nothing to add.'

Fredericks looked up from his pad at Rennie. 'For my benefit, Mr Rennie, perhaps you can tell me what this is all about.'

Rennie looked at Paynter but his face showed neither encouragement nor concern as he looked back at him. Rennie looked at Fredericks and said quietly, 'It'll be easier if I give you my report.'

Fredericks shrugged briefly. 'If that's what you want, Mr Rennie.'

'My team found out where Mason was being held but it wasn't possible to get him out without an actual attack on the place where he was being held. I was told from London that that was out.

'After a meeting in London with Mr Paynter it was concluded that the only way of getting Mason back was to put pressure on Khalim Said. And that the only pressure that would be effective was the kidnapping of his two young children. I was instructed – ordered – to go ahead and do that.

'This was done under my supervision, but only after some action against the kidnappers was Mason rescued and Said's children were returned to him. He has no proof that SIS was involved in kidnapping his children nor does he know how Mason was released. I debriefed Mason in Amsterdam and escorted him back to London two days ago.' Rennie leaned back in his chair. 'Those are the basic details. I'll be making a full report when I'm back at the office.'

Paynter said, 'There seems to . . .'

Fredericks silenced Paynter with a shake of his head and then looked across at Rennie.

'It sounds a well-planned and well-executed operation, Mr Rennie, if I might say so, as a mere bystander, so to speak. So tell me now why you want to be dissociated from it.'

For long moments Rennie sat silent and then, looking at Fredericks directly, he said, 'I've never disputed or even questioned an order from Mr Paynter or anyone else I have worked for in SIS. I didn't see it as either my role or within my status to question orders. But when it came to lifting the two children I was reluctant. Mr Paynter knows that. But when I was told to do it, I did it. I want to make clear that I'll never carry out an order in future that I find abhorrent. And if anybody wants my resignation they can have it right now.'

Fredericks spoke very quietly. 'I can imagine that this operation must have been a great strain on you, Mr Rennie. However, I don't think anybody should start leaping to decisions or making threats. You are a valuable and much respected member of your department, Mr Rennie, and your views will be borne in mind.' Fredericks paused. 'Am I right in thinking that it was the taking of the children that you disliked?'

'Yes. And the consequences.'

'What consequences, Mr Rennie? I took it that the children were back with their father, safe and sound.'

'Safe, Mr Fredericks, but not sound.'

'You'd better explain, perhaps.'

'They've gone to the States to get away from their memories of what happened. The little girl is in a mental hospital under the daily care of an analyst. I understand the technical term is "trauma". The Arab's marriage is virtually over.'

Paynter said angrily, 'For Christ's sake, Johnny. The Arab was in it up to his neck. It works both ways, you know. Kidnapping and threats are a dangerous operation. Sometimes the danger ends up coming back at you. He should have thought about his family before he got mixed up in it. It's all very well bemoaning your fate when it goes wrong on you. That's what they all do.'

Rennie made as if to stand up but Fredericks waved him

169

down. 'How about you have some leave, Rennie? Go and get some sun. Somewhere warm.'

'Have you finished with me, sir?'

'Of course.' Fredericks looked at Paynter. 'We have, haven't we?'

Paynter nodded, his face still flushed with anger. When Rennie had left, Fredericks said. 'It won't do to antagonise him. Let him cool off. You too. We'll have to think how to get him back into line.'

'A little harassment won't do Master Rennie any harm.'

'Maybe not, but you'd better not lean too heavily or you'll be getting a note of resignation on your desk some bright morning.'

Paynter stood up slowly. 'Maybe that's not a bad idea either. He's not going to be as useful to me in future whatever he does.'

'Oh come on. It was you who told me how good he was when I criticised him. One kick over the traces doesn't mean he's suddenly no good.'

'Maybe. Maybe not. Are your people satisfied with how it went?'

'They're not *my* people. I'm in both camps. Liaison not partisanship. All I do is act as a humble interpreter. One side to the other. But, yes. The FO are relieved that there were no diplomatic repercussions. I suggested an MBE for Rennie. The January list.' He smiled. ' "Services to foreign trade." '

Paynter only half-smiled as he walked to the door.

Chapter 22

IT WAS almost a week before Rennie got around to checking his mail. There was a pile of a dozen or so letters on the table and three letters that had been addressed to him at SIS's security Post Office box number. He opened those first.

One was a note from Finance asking for a meeting about his expenses in Holland; one was a slip confirming the tax-free payment of his salary cheque to the merchant bank; and the third was notification that he was due for an official medical.

The other mail was mainly bills and reminders. There were a few mail-shots offering pension schemes and one from a book-club with a special offer. The one that mattered was an official letter from his landlord giving him two months' notice to quit the flat. He put it aside for his solicitor to deal with. He was sure there was at least a year to go on his lease.

He phoned Macalister but he was in court and he made an appointment to see one of the other partners. He took a taxi to Regent Street and walked up to the third-floor reception. The girl phoned through to Mr Cooper and then pointed the way down the corridor. For a moment he thought he had heard the girl say 'Yes, Mr Macalister' on the telephone as he went through the swing doors.

Mr Cooper was young and dapper and he pointed to the chair in front of his desk.

'I understand that it's a lease problem, Mr Rennie?'

'Yes. But there shouldn't be a problem. The lease isn't up for another thirteen months.'

'May I see the lease and the letter?'

Rennie handed them to him and sat waiting as the solicitor read the contract then the letter. Eventually he looked up from the document at Rennie.

'The clause they quote – clause fourteen brackets three. You understand what that means?'

'It means the period of the letting. Two years in my case.'

'I'm afraid not. This is what's called a "periodic tenancy". The two years is the maximum period of tenancy. You pay your rent monthly, don't you?'

'Yes. But that was because the landlord said he preferred it that way.'

'I'm sure he does, but from that it follows that the landlord only needs to give you a month's notice to quit. Apart from that, according to the lease you accepted that the landlord was not a company but a person, and was a resident landlord.'

'He's just got a room upstairs.'

'Is it occupied?'

'Yes, there's a girl there. He stays there sometimes during the week.'

'Well I'm afraid that makes it even more difficult. If you try and contest it you could probably hang on for three months. But you'd end up paying his costs as well as your own. It's not worth it.'

'Is there any point in me having a word with Mr Macalister? He checked it over for me.'

Cooper shook his head. 'It wouldn't make any difference. The clause is there and you signed the lease.' He leaned back in his chair and stared at Rennie. 'Of course you could always sue us for negligence if you feel it wasn't done to your instructions.' He paused. 'I suspect it wouldn't succeed. But that's up to you.'

Rennie stood up and Cooper gave him back the documents and saw him to the door.

The medical took a day and a half of being attached to one instrument after another, and he had a psychiatric test and a long interview with a psychologist. They were all full-time SIS specialists. Medicals were compulsory and at random

172

intervals.

Rennie was dressed and waiting when the medical supervisor came in with his file.

'Don't stand up, please. I just want to go over a few things and have a word with you. By the way, are you operational at the moment?'

'No. I'm on leave.'

'Well now.' The supervisor looked at the notes pinned to the file cover. 'Physical fine. Muscle tone excellent, blood OK. But a couple of things. Your blood pressure is a bit over your normal and your reflexes are a bit slow. I'll give you a few pills to bring it down but the reflexes I'm afraid we can't help. They'll probably come back, but I suggest you take it easy for a month or two.' He put the file on the floor then his foot on the file as he leaned back to look at Rennie.

'I'm a bit worried about the psychiatrist's report. Have you got any pressures at the moment?'

'Just the usual pressures that anybody has.'

'Nothing more than that?'

'I don't think so.'

'The report says . . .' He watched Rennie's face as he spoke. '. . . "marked indecision" and "some indications of paranoia". What would you say about those comments?'

Rennie half-smiled and shrugged. 'I took a short psychology course during my training and I can remember being told that the classification of paranoia was not a matter of persecution complex as lay people call it, but of chronic symptoms of extraordinary behaviour from a feeling of being persecuted. So it seems unlikely that your chap can have observed me over a period long enough to describe anything as chronic. And I'd like to know what the extraordinary behaviour is that he's observed.'

The supervisor smiled. 'I'm afraid the misdescription was mine. I used paranoia in its lay sense – persecution complex. The psychologist merely noted that a number of your replies indicated a hidden resentment of something or other – possibly an overdone resentment of any form of criticism.'

Rennie shrugged. 'I never take too much notice of what

other people think of me. I worked out my own lifestyle a long time ago.'

The supervisor nodded. 'OK. Well, just bear it in mind.' He reached for a pad on his desk. 'I'll give you a prescription for the blood pressure. It looks a temporary thing, and it's certainly nothing to worry about.'

The following weekend he took the girls to the Planetarium on the Saturday afternoon, and when they returned to where he had parked his cár it had gone. He reported the theft to the police and gave them his name, address and telephone number.

They were playing rummy that evening when the police called him and told him that his car had not been stolen but towed away for causing an obstruction. He would have to claim it personally at the Elephant and Castle police pound. It was not manned on a Sunday so it would not be available until Monday morning. He hung up and sat there for several minutes before the girls called him back to get on with the game. Two days earlier his car had been festooned with three different parking tickets.

After paying the fine and claiming the car Rennie spent the Monday and Tuesday at Century House working on his day-by-day report on the Amsterdam operation. He phoned Paynter on the internal phone several times but he wasn't available.

On the Wednesday evening he ate a snack at the Special Forces Club and then strolled back to the flat down Sloane Street towards Sloane Square. As he waited for some cars to pass before crossing the road to Peter Jones a girl asked him how to get to the Markham Arms. He was not a frequenter of pubs and there were several in the King's Road so he hesitated as he tried to work out which one was the Markham Arms. As the girl stood there waiting for an answer a man touched his arm and as he turned to look at him the man showed him an identity card. 'Sergeant Davies, mister. Vice Squad. I'm charging you under the Justices of the Peace Act. Breaching the peace.'

Rennie reached in his pocket and brought out his own

identity card. 'My name's Rennie. This is my ID card. I'm afraid you've got the wrong person.'

The man shook his head. 'That won't help you, sir. I'm still charging you.'

'For what?'

'Like I said – breaching the peace. Accosting WPC Coleman for sex.' And he pointed at the girl.

'You must be out of your mind, sergeant. She merely asked me how to get to one of the pubs in King's Road.'

'You'll have an opportunity of telling the magistrates your version of events, Mr Rennie. Meantime I'd like your full name and address please.'

Paynter was available the first time he called him the following morning, and Rennie wondered what his reaction would be. He seemed amiable and friendly, talking on the phone as he waved Rennie to a chair. As he hung up he looked across at Rennie, smiling.

'Sorry I've been so elusive the last few days. My girl says you've phoned several times. I thought you were on leave.'

'I am, officially. I wanted to get my log over and done with.'

'Don't fret about it, Johnny. You're more important to us than a bloody report.' He smiled. 'Fredericks tells me that the FO have approved a rather nice little surprise for you next January one.'

'Thanks. But if that means what I think it means then there are problems.'

'What are the problems? Maybe we can help sort them out.'

Rennie told him about the encounter with the police and the problem concerning his flat. Paynter noted down names, addresses and telephone numbers and dates, and leaned back in his chair. 'Leave it to me, Johnny. We'll teach those bastards a lesson. The Met *and* the landlord. Believe me, their feet won't touch.' He stood up. 'Forget it. All of it. Leave it to your uncle. When you're part of the family as you are they ain't gonna play games and get away with it. The cheeky bastards. I've got to push off now, I'm afraid. Trouble in Brazil. Old Lawson's got his knickers in a twist and we've got to organise some help. Call me tomorrow about three. And I'll tell you what I've done.'

Rennie had just come back from the canteen when Paynter walked into his office and pulled up a chair. He looked at some notes on a card as he spoke.

'Abject apologies from the Metropolitan Police. They've been doing a blitz on kerb-crawlers and others in the Sloane Square area. Afraid that it was going to become a new spot for girls. Sergeant Davies has been kicked up the arse for being over-enthusiastic and the record's been wiped out. So that's that.' Paynter turned over the card. 'Your landlord would be very happy for you to stay the full term of your lease at the present rental.' Paynter grinned at Rennie. 'He felt his wife might not be too happy if she heard about the little bird who he keeps in his place up the stairs.'

Paynter tore up the card, searched for the wastepaper basket and threw the pieces away. Then he looked at Rennie, smiling as he stood up. 'There aren't many benefits we get in the old firm but putting on a bit of pressure where it counts is something we *can* do.'

Chapter 23

PAYNTER STOOD on the steps of the Reform with Fredericks and watched the rain lashing down.

Fredericks turned and said, 'Let's go back inside and have a coffee until it's cleared. I'll ring for a pool car to pick us up.'

They sat on the balcony and a club servant brought the coffee things on a tray, and as Paynter poured, Fredericks said, 'I gather your little scheme worked with friend Rennie.'

'Yes. No problem. It always works. A bit of pressure and then the magic wand.'

'You don't think he rumbled what was going on? He's an old hand. Probably seen it happen to others.'

Paynter grinned. 'That's the beauty of it. If they don't cotton on to what's happening they're impressed and grateful for what we do for them. And the relief of everything going back to normal. If they *do* suspect that it's a put-up job it gives them pause to think. If that's what can happen just as a warning, what might happen if it was for real? If they're clever enough to work it out, they get the message. Loud and clear. Play ball and life goes on its merry way. Play silly buggers and they need to keep wondering when the next load of bricks is going to drop on them.'

Fredericks sipped his coffee and then, leaning forward, he said, 'The odd thing is that I'd have bet my last pound on you never needing to do that sort of thing to Rennie. He's never questioned anything, and God knows you've given him some pretty rough assignments in the last few years.'

'I agree. His attitude was always that what happened to the opposition was exactly what they deserved. And he was the department's avenging angel seeing that they got their just desserts.' He shrugged. 'Ah well. It's a lesson learned. For me as well as him.' He smiled. 'Like the Bible says, "Put not your trust in princes, nor in any child of man: for there is no help in them." '

Fredericks half-smiled. 'The Book of Common Prayer, actually. I should keep him in London for a bit if I were you. Easier to keep an eye on him.'

'True.'

'Ah. There's Grainger with the car, let's get going.'

Although Paynter had been close to Rennie for years and had frequently defended his unquestioning loyalty against criticism from SIS's intellectuals, he had totally misread Rennie's reaction to the minor harassments that had been used to bring him to heel. Rennie had been suspicious when his car had collected so many parking tickets and then finally been towed away. When the Metropolitan Police had been used to pressure him by invoking an Act of Parliament drawn up in 1361 his suspicions were confirmed. When he went to Paynter it was a piece of routine so far as Rennie was concerned. He was neither disturbed by what they had done nor concerned about what else would be done. It was a routine response to a move in an official game of chess. It was a nuisance that he wanted to put a stop to. When the department had 'put things right' that would be the end of the matter. That was how they worked. He had to seem grateful for their help or worried about what might happen if he didn't toe the line. But he wasn't grateful, he was resentful at being treated to such a juvenile charade. But if that was what they wanted he was willing to go along with the ritual until he had worked out what he wanted to do. It was no more than a minor irritation compared with his own growing torment of doubt.

Rennie was never aware before of dreaming but his sleep now was fitful and disturbed. Disturbed by dreams of his childhood and his father, and sometimes he dreamed of things he had done, men he had killed, men he had pressured to breaking point. They weren't nightmares. They no more frightened him now than the actual events had done. What disturbed him was that they were uncontrollable. He could neither avoid them nor stop them. They just happened. And always there was the face of Paynter somewhere in the dream. Not menacing but smiling. An amused smile. Not part of the incident but an observer of the dream.

In his rational daytime thoughts Rennie tried to separate his doubts. His continued doubts about himself, and his doubts about his attitude to Paynter and the department. Perhaps they were right and, like they said, all he needed was a rest in the sun. And the things he did had to be done by someone. The Americans, the French, the Germans, the Arabs and the Israelis – they all had people who did those things. They were heroes not villains. They risked their lives just as he did, for their country. The world had changed, diplomacy was no longer enough. The moment one country started the rough stuff the others had to respond. They may wish, like the British, that they didn't have to, but if they didn't they'd go down into anarchy or surrender. International politics had become a jungle where only the fit and ruthless survived. The things he did were to hold the ring so that governments and diplomats could negotiate and manoeuvre and make it look as if civilisation still mattered.

If his thinking on all this was wrong then what was left? This had been his life for too long to be able to just walk out. And what would he do? How would he earn a living? And where would Paynter find a replacement? It took years of experience to be able to do the things he did, efficiently and purposefully. He may not owe Paynter anything personally, but what about his loyalty to the things Paynter represented? You can't just walk away from your country and all that it represents. Decency, tolerance, democracy and all the other vague things that he cared about. That picture that he always kept in his mind: all those young people singing 'Land of Hope and Glory' at the last night of the Proms. That was what it was all about. He would be rejecting all of them too.

A dozen times a day he rationalised his thoughts until

there were no doubts left. He would carry on as he always had. Loyal to the things he believed in. But no sooner was the decision made than his thoughts went back to Khalim Said and his wife and the little girl. He could take a deep breath and accept that it was just one of those unfortunate things that happen when a man like Said gets mixed up in matters that he doesn't really understand. And for God's sake, surely Said was old enough and sophisticated enough to realise what he was doing. Why should *he* be immune to the consequences of what he put his hand to? What right did he have to expect that there would be no day of reckoning or that his family would not be involved? He had gone to Paris deliberately to check on Mason. He had slept with Mason's wife. Not even out of desire or lust, but cold-bloodedly, just to check that he was what the fanatics wanted. Where was the dignity and Islamic justification for that? The thoughts about Khalim Said were only fleeting elusive thoughts but they always seemed enough to crumble his resolve to indecision again.

Rennie was well aware that Fredericks and some of the others saw him as no more than a thug. A ruthless thug who was respected or tolerated only because of his being on their side. But Rennie was indifferent to what they thought. He knew where he stood. The people he fought were men of evil and Rennie saw evil as being an actuality. Evil was as real as goodness. As positive as virtue. As definable as any other human characteristic.

What made that evil in the first place was no concern of his. His only concern was that evil should be vanquished. Cleanly, ruthlessly as a surgeon's knife removes a malignant growth from an otherwise healthy body. It was not romantic. He was not a knight in shining armour, he was the protector of all those ordinary people who had no idea of the forces ranged against them. The subversives who worked in every field to bring the country to ruin. The assassins who murdered and then looked to British courts for justice and mercy. The abusers of society. The infiltrators who so crudely turned striking workers into a fighting rabble and then complained about the police interfering with their 'democratic' rights.

Back on duty Paynter briefed him on the details of an MP who was being set up by a small group of Greek Cypriots. The Cypriots weren't looking for a protagonist in the Commons – the MP was also the owner and chairman of an electronics company which designed and manufactured components for surface-to-air missiles. The Greek Cypriots were planning a free-enterprise and 'unofficial' strike against the Turkish aircraft that zoomed lazily in and out of the northern half of Cyprus that the Turks had invaded and occupied. The missiles would jack up the stakes high enough to make the UN take notice of their government's case. They had the missiles already but they didn't know how to operate them. But there were several men employed by Roger Lumley who could teach them how.

The SIS evaluation was that the Cypriots had come to the conclusion that money wouldn't work – Lumley was making a pile on contracts for the British government and half a dozen others including Egypt and Brazil. Ill-informed, they had gone off on a wild-goose chase through gossip from a Cypriot waiter at the restaurant he regularly used. Gossip had suggested that Roger Lumley was homo-sexual. And gossip had been wrong. A patriotic young Cypriot was now nursing a badly bruised face and a gap in his teeth. Roger Lumley had been a divisional welterweight champion during his army service.

Special Branch had better sources of Cypriot and Greek gossip than the ill-assorted group and had watched with passing interest the machinations of the patriots holed up in one room over a topless bar in D'Arblay Street in Soho. For some administrative reason the operation had been passed over by MI5 to SIS.

'What we're interested in,' Paynter said, 'is not pulling in this gang of amateurs but keeping tabs on Lumley. They'll keep on at him because their masters have told them to, and we'd like to see how Lumley reacts when they find out the chink in his armour.'

'Any idea what the chink might be?'

Paynter shrugged. 'Five seem to think they were on the right lines with sex. But girls not boys.'

'Why? It seems a bit obvious and traditional.'

'Yes. If he was just an industrialist it wouldn't matter. But against an MP they can use sex things more easily. The poor bastard would have all the usual hassle with the media. Local party chairman swearing eternal loyalty and then the committee meetings where the other contenders for the seat put the knife in for the sake of the morals of the constituency. The poor sod always loses out in the end. Anyway, it's an interesting exercise. Should keep you going for a couple of months.'

'Why don't they go down the line a bit and use one of Lumley's technicians?'

'I'd guess for several reasons. Like I said, an MP is still open to blackmail. He may wish he could defy them but he knows that as an MP the scandal will finish him no matter how it ends up.

'And a technician can't just swan off to Ankara or Famagusta just for the hell of it. No – they're right in going for Lumley. He's a sitting duck once they've got something on him.'

'Is this a solo or do I have a team?'

'Well, start solo and see me if you feel it's worth expanding a bit. There's a name in the file. A Ministry of Defence bod who knows Lumley well. Could be useful as a lead to meeting Lumley.'

It was two weeks later when Fredericks phoned Paynter to see him in his office. As Paynter sat down Fredericks passed him a page from a magazine.

'Have you seen that? It's an early copy of this week's *Newsweek*. Washington sent it over in last night's bag. Don't read it all now. Just the bit that's side-lined.'

Paynter turned the page the right way round and read the two paragraphs that had been marked with an orange highlighter.

. . . no doubt the debate in Congress will include some voices asking if nothing was learned from the shambles of Watergate and the 'dirty tricks' department of the

CIA.

Rumour has it that even England's usually discreet MI6 is not above taking a leaf from the CIA books. Recent unreported MI6 operations in the Netherlands and Australia bear an uncanny likeness to the pre-Watergate habits of our own intelligence services. Old habits certainly die hard so far as 'dirty tricks' are concerned.

There is also the question of whether such operations receive an official 'blind eye' or . . .

Paynter looked up as he finished reading.

'Just fishing, I'd say. Seeing if anyone rises to the bait. And the thing in Australia was ASIO not us.'

'No consultation with us? No advice?' Fredericks's voice was sharp.

'Not officially anyway. And certainly nothing in writing.'

'And the Netherlands reference?'

'Could be a shot in the dark.'

'Oh come on. Who the hell has been up to anything in the Netherlands in the last four years that could reasonably be described as dirty tricks? Somebody's talked and I know who I suspect.'

'Who?'

For the first time in years Paynter saw Fredericks lose his temper. His voice cracking with anger. 'Don't bullshit *me*, Paynter. I have to respond to this piece. What do you expect me to do?'

'Say it's a shot in the dark.'

'You must be out of your mind. I've personally put my name to a recommendation for an MBE for Rennie in the next Honours List.'

'Did you say what it was for?'

'Of course I bloody well did. They're not given out with the rations despite what the public thinks. I didn't give details but I mentioned a very delicate operation in Amsterdam.' He paused. 'And only a few weeks back the chap was sitting right here in this office saying he wanted to be dissociated from the operation.' Fredericks paused. 'Has he put in his resignation like he threatened?'

'No. He hasn't even mentioned it again. I put that bit of mild harassment on him and he came into line. He was just strung up from the operation.'

'Rennie's not the kind who gets strung-up from operations. You know that as well as I do. You were always on about his loyalty and dependability. You wished you had more like him. Remember?'

'Have you borne in mind that it could be somebody else? Khalim Said for instance.'

'I read Rennie's full report. According to that Said had got troubles enough of his own, and apart from that Rennie was sure that Said never connected him with SIS. Said's got too much to lose by talking about that affair.'

'Do you want me to do a discreet internal check before I take action against Rennie? There were others involved, you know.'

'Look, Hugo. I've never trusted Rennie. You know my views on him. He's a ruthless, tough bastard and you've found him useful. But you were just as surprised as I was when he put on his little act in this office, disassociating himself from the operation. You were sure you knew him inside out, but you were wrong. He's a loner and he doesn't lay his cards down on the table. I didn't trust him way back and I don't trust him now. You can say I'm prejudiced and maybe I am. But I'm right as well. So let's stop playing games.'

'What do you want me to do?'

Fredericks leaned forward and said quietly, 'I want you to put the real bite on that bastard. Show him that if he breathes one word out of place he's going to get the full treatment. And put somebody on to keeping an eye on him. Not a team. He'd spot that. But give him the works.'

'What will you tell the FO people?'

'That's my worry. You just do your part and don't let the bastard make any more waves than he has done already.'

'Do you want me to confront him about this piece?'

'Oh Jesus. No, no, no.' Fredericks' anger overflowed. 'Just do what I've told you. And keep me in touch, especially if you have any doubts.'

'I'll do that.'

184

Chapter 24

PAYNTER SAT in the first-floor coffee place at the Hilton and watched Mason getting out of the lift. He still looked pale and unwell but Paynter needed to keep the Amsterdam operation in as closed a circle as he could. And that meant using Mason.

He smiled amiably as Mason shed his coat and sat down at the table.

'What'll you have?' He had in mind coffee or tea but he hid his annoyance as Mason asked for a Bloody Mary. He realised that Mason looked a Bloody Mary type. A bit on the wet side despite his good looks. When the drink had been brought he pulled his chair nearer to Mason's.

'I've got a bit of a problem, Mason. I need your help.'

Mason smiled. 'Glad to be wanted. I've felt a bit spare and unloved since I got back.'

'Well, that's natural. But oddly enough the problem comes out of that business in Amsterdam.'

Mason pursed his lips. 'Not my favourite place, Amsterdam.'

'I'm sure it isn't. But the problem's here in London. Your friend Rennie as a matter of fact.'

Mason sighed. 'I don't think he sees me as a friend these days. I'm a bit of a broken reed in his eyes.'

Paynter ignored the plea and went on. 'There was a piece in one of the American magazines. Mainly about dirty tricks in the CIA but it made a fleeting mention of SIS and dirty tricks. It specifically mentioned a recent SIS operation in the Netherlands.'

'Good grief. Now what?'

'Now nothing. If we can keep the lid on it. But Rennie

turned a bit wet about the Amsterdam operation. Has he said anything to you?'

'No. He's avoided me. But I know he was put out about the Arab's kid and the wife. I think he had in mind that sort of thing happening to his own daughters.'

'Did he now? Did he say that?'

'No. But when he was debriefing me, before I got back here, it was obvious that it stuck in his gullet. Made him a bit sharp with me. Because I talked.'

'I see. Anyway, we're worried that he might have leaked the story because he didn't like what he had to do.'

Mason shook his head, frowning. 'That isn't the kind of thing Rennie would do. I'd stake my life on that. He's dead straight, is Rennie. If he wanted to raise hell he'd do it head on.'

'You sound like a Rennie fan. Are you?'

'I suppose I am in a way. I admire him. He's tough and he's got bags of courage. Never seen him back down. And in his own peculiar way he's straight as a die.'

'You may be right. Maybe he didn't leak. But somebody did. And I want you to keep an eye on Rennie for me. I'm going to post you to him as an assistant on the job he's doing now.'

Mason shrugged. 'If that's what you want.'

'I'll notify him tomorrow.'

Mason nodded and finished his drink. And then Paynter remembered.

'How's things with your wife now? Any progress?'

There were tears at the edges of Mason's eyes, as always at any mention of his wife, but he brushed them away with the back of his hand. 'She's started the divorce. I wanted to defend it but Legal said no. It could mean things coming out in court or using the Official Secrets Act to prevent it. They didn't want either to happen.'

'Is there anything we could do? Explain to her that it was only your work kept you away?'

'She knows it was that. But she's not the kind of girl who goes for that sort of stuff. And she's French not British, despite the passport. It's gone too far. I've had it so far as she's concerned.'

186

'I'm sorry. Very sorry. Maybe you'll meet someone else with more understanding. I hope so. And you're a good-looking chap, you know,'

Mason half-smiled. 'I don't want anyone else. I want her.'

'I understand.' He stood up. 'I'll contact you tomorrow when I've spoken to Rennie.' He paused. 'Can I give you a lift anywhere?'

'No. I'll hang on here for a bit and have another noggin.'

Rennie had been formal but not unfriendly when Mason reported to him.

'There's not much happening, Mason. It's a bit of a wild-goose chase in my opinion, but a new face will be useful. I've been in every porn shop in Soho trying to keep an eye on these birds.' He smiled. 'I think whoever's backing them and funding them is being taken for a ride.'

'What are they like?'

'A pretty hairy bunch. There's one smoothie who wears the good clothes. He's trying to get alongside Lumley's secretary at the moment. She's in her fifties. The old retainer. Been with him for years but I think the Cypriot's making some progress all the same. Her cleaning lady's from Cyprus and he's doing the dutiful nephew bit.'

Rennie took Mason to see the various cafes and clubs frequented by the Cypriots, and drove him over to see the outside of Lumley's plant on the industrial estate on Purley Way. They also drove past the small semi-detached house in Waddon where Lumley's secretary lived. As they drove off Mason said, 'Is Lumley married?'

'Yes. But not very happily from what I've heard. She's a bit of a virago. But they keep up appearances.'

'Is he likely to fall for girl-bait?'

'Guessing, I'd say yes. He's got a thing for very young girls. He has sex with a girl in the typing pool at his works – looks like strictly business for both parties. And he also finances a young married woman who lives in South Croydon. She used to work for him and he visits her frequently in the daytime. If it was carefully done I'd say he'd fall all right.'

'Any signs of them finding a suitable girl?'

'Well, they've had dozens of girls at their rooms in Soho. All young and pretty. Those we've been able to identify are Maltese or Cypriots and they may be looking them over for pushing at Lumley. One of the prettiest is definitely a hooker. But I'd guess they'd all play if there was incentive enough. They'd be able to offer her a chance to be a patriot and earn a few quid at the same time. Their problem is getting her alongside Lumley. But he has been known to visit one or two shady clubs in Soho. Shouldn't be too difficult to get them together but not so easy to raise the proposition about the missiles.'

'Anything you'd like me to do tomorrow?'

'Yes. See if you can put together a list of the chaps at Lumley's place who are capable of showing those goons how to fire a missile. Take your time on it but keep in touch, even if it's only a nil report.'

'OK. Where shall I contact you?'

'Office or flat, it doesn't matter.'

Back at the office there was a message on Rennie's desk to ring his wife as soon as possible.

Rennie rang several times but there was no reply. He looked at his watch. It was nearly six and they ought to be there. It was a schoolday and homework to be done. He decided that he'd drive over and see what she wanted. And it was a chance to see the girls.

It was dark when he pulled up at the house and there were no lights on in any of the windows. He rang the bell and waited. But there was no response. He walked round to the back of the house. The curtains weren't drawn and the house was obviously empty. Walking back to the porch he opened his wallet and took out the small slip of plastic, hesitated and then put it back. It might be legally his house but he wasn't entitled to break in.

There were lights on in the houses on both sides. He decided on the Crasters. Craster was something in banking or insurance and had always nodded when he had seen

Rennie picking up the girls. It was Craster himself who answered the door.

'Hello, old man. What can I do for you?'

'I had a message to phone my ex-wife as soon as possible. I couldn't get an answer so I came over. But the place is empty. I wondered if you knew where they were.'

'I don't I'm afraid. But hold on. Fran might know.' He turned and called out, 'Fran.'

She was wiping her hands on a teacloth as she hurried down the hall.

'What is it, Frankie? Oh hello. Mr Rennie, isn't it?'

Craster said, 'Wondered if you knew where Mrs Rennie and the girls are. She phoned him to contact her but there's nobody there.'

Mrs Craster looked intently at Rennie's face. 'It's not some domestic quarrel, is it?'

'Fran . . .' Craster said angrily, '. . . whatever next. How can you say such a thing? Mr Rennie and . . .'

'Be quiet, Frank.' She turned to Rennie. 'She was very upset about something. She fetched the girls from school at lunch-time and I saw them leave about an hour later in a taxi. They had suitcases with them. She looked terribly agitated.'

'Which direction did the taxi go?'

Mrs Craster pointed. 'Down towards the main street. I hope she's not poorly.'

'Would you allow me to use your telephone? She might have gone to her mother's.'

Craster waved him inside. 'Of course. Come in.' He pointed towards the glass-topped table. 'Help yourself. Give us a call when you've finished.'

Mrs Winfield, Mary's mother, had been shocked by the divorce. She was a staunch admirer of Rennie, and with Mary not wanting her mother to know about her lapse with Cowley the explanations had been unconvincing. But she still sent him cards at Christmas and on his birthday. He dialled the number and after several rings he heard her quavering voice.

'Who is that?'

'It's Johnny, mother. Is Mary with you?'

He heard the phone clatter at the other end and then his ex-wife's breathless voice. She was almost whispering.

'Is that you, Johnny?'

'Yes. What's going on? I got a message to ring you. I got no answer so I . . .'

'Johnny. I'm scared.'

'Of what?'

'Can you come over,' she whispered. 'I don't want the girls to hear.'

'You mean come over now, tonight?'

'Yes. Please come, Johnny. Please help me.'

'Of course I will. Just relax and I'll be there in about forty-five minutes.'

He hung up and called out to the Crasters, told them that Mary was at her mother's and headed for his car.

Mrs Winfield lived in a detached house in Purley, near where he had been with Mason earlier that day when they were looking at Lumley's factory. There were lights on all over the house and as he walked up the garden path Mary was standing at the open door. She looked pale, and even in the dim light he could see that she had been crying.

'Oh Johnny. Thank God you've come. I've been out of my mind all day. I phoned but you were out. Don't go in, the girls are still up.'

'Tell me what's the matter,' Rennie said quietly.

'I fainted, Johnny. I've never fainted in my life before.'

'Let's walk round the block. Leave the door.'

'Is it safe, d'you think?'

'Of course it is. Come on.'

He waited until they were several houses away and then stopped by a street light and turned her so that he could look at her. Her whole body was shaking.

'Now tell me what's happened.'

'I took the girls to school and was back just after nine. About ten there was a knock on the door. When I opened it there were two men there, a young one and an old one. And there was a van in the road. I asked them what they wanted and the older man took off his hat and said he'd brought the coffins. I think I was kind of dazed and I said I didn't understand. He said to come and look, and I went out to the van. There were three coffins there on a strip of foam. A large one and two small ones . . .' She burst into tears and he put his hands on her shoulders.

'Go on, Mary.'

She took a deep breath as she looked up at his face. 'They had labels on them. Glued on. One said, "Mary Rennie" and the others just said "Elizabeth" and "Mary". I walked back to the house and the old man came with me. He gave me an envelope. There was a note inside. It was typed, and it said "Be very quiet and very careful". I looked at it and I must have passed out. When I came to I was in the kitchen and the old man was wiping my face with a cloth. He was very concerned. I told him to take the coffins away. That it was all a mistake.'

'Where's the note?'

'I don't know. I looked for it afterwards but I couldn't find it.'

'Go on.'

'I phoned you and left the message and I didn't know what to do. I panicked and phoned mother. She said come over and I fetched the girls from school. They helped me pack and I called a taxi and we came over.'

'Did you tell the girls what had happened?'

'Oh God, no. But they could see I was worried and they're terribly upset. Was I a fool about it all?'

'No. Of course not. People play these tricks from time to time. Practical jokes. But they're not very funny for the folk on the receiving end. I'll come back in and chat to the girls. Wipe your eyes and tell them it was a stupid joke by one of my friends. Go back home when you feel like it. It won't happen again. I'll sort out whoever's done this idiotic thing.'

'But who would do such a terrible thing. It's the kind of thing gangsters do to one another in New York, isn't it?'

Rennie smiled. 'More like Chicago. Don't worry about who did it. I'll soon find out and there'll be no such nonsense again.'

She smiled up at him. 'You know, you're a good man, Johnny Rennie. A real rock.' She hunched her shoulders. 'Let's go in. I feel fine all of a sudden.'

Rennie stayed until after ten, playing Scrabble with the two girls and afterwards reading them a story in bed. They caught the relief of their mother and grandmother and were back to normal long before they went to bed. Mrs Winfield gave him a thermos of coffee to take with him and was obviously relieved that all had turned out well in the end.

It took Rennie an hour and a half to find Mason's place in Pimlico. He had the top floor of a Victorian house in one of the rundown streets off the Embankment. It was several minutes before Mason opened the door. He was wearing just an old blue shirt and a pair of slippers, standing there unsteadily, trying to work out who it was. Rennie could smell the booze on his breath. Then Mason said slowly, slurring his words, 'Well hello, Johnny. The balloon gone up? Third World War and all that?'

'Can I come in, Mason?'

'By all means. Welcome to my humble abode.'

Mason staggered slightly as he drew out a chair by the table and sat down heavily opposite Rennie.

'A drinkie, old man?'

'No thanks. I need your help, Mason. Will you listen carefully while I explain.'

'Something serious is it?'

'Important to me anyway.'

Mason stood up, swaying slightly. 'In that case let me dip the old head in a drop of cold water. Let's clear the brain for action, eh?'

Five minutes later Mason came back. His face ruddy, hair combed, and wearing an ancient bath-robe, He moved sharply and seemed to have recovered.

'Forgive the shambles and the stupor. What's cooking?'

'Can this be between just you and me?'

'Of course it can.'

'Is that a promise?'

Mason half-smiled. 'Do you trust my promises, Johnny?'

'Yes. Why shouldn't I?'

'I'm the man who talked, remember? One twist of my balls and I called it a day. You debriefed me so you know all about it. No hero me. No stiff upper lip. Just a couple of screams and I blew the gaff.'

'Harry, you were in no fit state to resist anyone. You'd already been through the mincer with Fleur in Paris.'

Mason sighed and then said softly, 'She was very beautiful, Johnny. And I loved her very much. It did influence me. I felt the department had caused my troubles. I begged them for a home posting. Just for a year to give me time with her. But no. They wouldn't. I didn't feel I owed the department all that much loyalty.'

'I met Fleur when I was trying to find you. She *is* beautiful. But like I told you before, being with her wouldn't have solved the problem. I'm not just guessing. I know.'

'How do you know?'

'I fell in love with a Fleur when I was first in the army. In the end I walked away. I knew we'd never last.'

'Why?'

'She was much younger than me. And very beautiful. Even priests turned their heads to have another look. We both thought we loved one another, but I knew in my heart that we didn't fit.'

'Why not?'

'I was jealous of other men. Every man. Old men, her uncles, passing strangers. The lot. She knew I was jealous and I think she liked it. But she did nothing to calm me down. She knew she was beautiful and she knew that all men found her attractive. We got engaged and I thought that would change it all. It didn't of course. She was out with a couple of men behind my back. One was my company commander. Both men were married so there was nothing in it for her except the conquest.' Rennie smiled. 'I sat down one night and wrote myself an "appreciation report", as if it was some campaign I was in. Typical army thinking. There was no doubt about the conclusion. There was nothing in it for me. Not a damn thing. So I walked out. I was desperately unhappy for a week. Terribly tempted to phone her. But after a week I realised it was a relief. I felt normal again.'

'And you've never regretted it?'

'No way. Just faintly embarrassed that I ever got into it in the first place.'

Mason leaned forward, looking at Rennie. 'You can't have liked telling me this. The guy who's got his lifestyle all worked out. The black and white man. No greys.'

'I've told you because I know you'll understand. And it might help you. I've never told anyone else.'

'Thanks for telling me.' He sighed heavily. 'Sometimes when I've been on my little treadmill thinking about Fleur I've thought exactly the same. And for an hour or so I feel relieved to be out of it. No more jealousy. No more imagining her with other men. Maybe it'll go in the end.'

'It will, Harry. It will. I promise.'

'We were talking about promises. Yes, I promise, Johnny.'

Rennie took a deep breath. 'When I came back from Amsterdam I told Paynter that I didn't like the kidnapping of Said's children and the consequences. They put on a little harassment to keep me in line. I went through the "help me" ritual and it was all stopped. But it's started again. I don't know why. But this time it's for real.' He paused. 'Three coffins were delivered at my ex-wife's house today. One had her name on it and the other two were in the names of my daughters. My wife was half out of her mind.'

Mason shook his head in disbelief. 'The shits.' He sighed. 'I know why they're doing it.'

'Tell me.'

'You won't let on that I told you?'

'This is just between you and me, like I said. It applies both ways. Me as well as you.'

'There was a piece in an American magazine. About the CIA and dirty tricks and there was a brief dig at an SIS dirty tricks operation in the Netherlands. It only came in two or three days ago. They think you leaked it to the press. Did you?'

'Of course I didn't. I never meet any press people anyway. I haven't told anyone outside the people concerned in the department.'

'Paynter told me about it. I said it wasn't you. What are you going to do?'

'I'm putting in my resignation tonight. It'll be on Paynter's desk in the morning.'

'For God's sake, Johnny. That'll make things worse. They'll do their nuts in case you talk any more.'

'That's their worry. As far as I'm concerned I've had enough. I don't trust them any more. Not their honour, nor their integrity, nor their motives. I wouldn't lift a finger for them ever again.'

'Would you talk?'

'No. Definitely not. Not unless they really put me in a corner.'

'What do you want me to do?'

'I think they've worked out that my dislike of what had to be done to Said's children shows where my Achilles' heel is. My family. That's why we had today's little game. I want to ask if you'll keep an eye on Mary and the two girls for me. Will you do that?'

'Yes. Of course I will.'

Rennie took out a card from his jacket pocket and handed it to Mason. 'I've put down various telephone numbers where you should be able to contact me.'

'Do you want to kip down here for the night?'

'Thanks, but I've got things to do before I sleep.'

Rennie typed out the brief letter of resignation on his portable and read it again and again before he signed it.

To: Paynter G.S. Dir. Sp. Services
From: Rennie J.H.

With this letter I give the required thirty-one days' notice of my resignation from SIS. With accumulated leave amounting to forty days I suggest that the department accepts that leave in lieu of both notice and attendance at H.Q.

J.H. Rennie.

It was almost three o'clock in the morning when he drove

to Century House. Showing his card at the security checks he made his way up to his office.

As he sat at his desk he unhooked the two keys from his key-ring and tucked them into an official envelope. Paynter's office and his secretary's office were both locked and Rennie left the two envelopes with the security guard in the outer office.

Back at the flat he undressed slowly and lay on the bed, wide-awake, trying to slow down his brain as the pictures and words of the day crowded and jostled obscenely in his mind.

He had never imagined such a situation and he was mentally unprepared. One half of his mind was totally in control. He wanted no more of such people. The other half was a confused observer of the shambles. Barely believing what was happening and vaguely fearful of what the outcome would be.

Rennie was not a man used to doubts. The action of writing out his resignation and delivering it had relieved his tension momentarily, but now it was done he realised that he had no idea what he was going to do next. The whole framework of his life had just gone. Not with a burst of gunfire or the flash of a knife as it went for his ribs, but just melted away like the fade-out at the end of a film. The adrenalin had been used up and his whole body ached as if he had been in a fight. He could feel the lethargy of exhaustion taking hold of his body and mind. He wanted to rouse himself, get up and start taking decisive action. But there was no will to move and no action to take.

It was the phone ringing that woke him. He looked at his watch. It was eleven-thirty. As he picked up the phone it all flooded back as he heard Paynter's voice. Amiable and calm. Would he pop in during the afternoon just to clear up a few things. The Lumley business, his pension and so on. He arranged to see Paynter at four.

Chapter 25

PAYNTER SAW him not in his office, but in one of the small conference rooms on the top floor. Rennie suspected that the room had been chosen because it was wired for recording. He saw no signs of mikes or switches but that didn't mean a thing.

Paynter came bustling in, Rennie's letter of resignation in his hand. He sat facing Rennie, smiling as he looked at him.

'You don't mean this, Johnny, do you? You're just having me on. Making a point.'

'I may be making a point but don't kid yourself about me meaning it. I mean it all right.'

Still looking amiable Paynter said, 'Is there anything – anything at all – that I can do to dissuade you? It'll be a real blow to the department to lose you. Nobody's irreplaceable but you're as near irreplaceable as you can get.'

Rennie shook his head decisively and Paynter was aware of the anger in Rennie's eyes.

'Well – if that's how you feel. I've checked with Finance. You'll be entitled to a pension of four-fifths of present salary. It becomes subject to tax, I'm afraid, but it *is* index-linked. That's some consolation.'

Rennie made to stand up and Paynter said, 'I really am sorry about all this, Johnny. Are you sure you're all right? How was your medical?'

'OK.'

'What if I suggested six months' leave on full pay?'

'I'd tell you to stuff it.'

Paynter pulled a face. 'Well in that case all I can say is thanks for all you've done and good luck for the future.' He paused. 'But I'd be very remiss if I didn't tell you that we're all very concerned about the state you've been in for the last few weeks.'

'Is that all?'

'Yes.'

Paynter put out his hand and Rennie ignored it, turning and walking to the door without looking back.

He saw Mason downstairs by the desk. He looked worried as Rennie walked over to him.

'How did you get on with Paynter? He told me you'd resigned. Seemed to accept it. Sad loss but you were rather disturbed at the moment.'

'He did accept it. A bit of soft soap but not aggressive.'

'Don't worry. I'll keep an eye on the family if you're not available. Any idea what you're going to do?'

'No. I haven't given it a thought as yet.'

'You won't have any problem getting a job with some big company, not with your experience.'

'I hope you're right.'

Rennie phoned Mary and mentioned Harry Mason as help if he was not around when she called, and reassured her that there would be no more trouble like yesterday's.

He was uneasy about his meeting with Paynter. He had gone there prepared for threats and bluster and a bit of table thumping, but Paynter had been reasonable enough bearing in mind the circumstances. Maybe he *was* a bit strung-up at the moment and not thinking straight. But instinct told him otherwise, and all his training and experience led him to trust his highly-developed animal instincts rather than logic or contradictory facts.

For two days he dealt with his accumulated bills and tidied his rooms. He read the 'Situations Vacant' ads in *The Times* and the *Daily Telegraph* but not with any great interest. He could live quite well enough on his pension. And like most SIS field agents he had lived virtually free of all expense and had money in several foreign banks. If it wasn't for the two girls he'd move to Spain or buy a boat and live on board. Cruising the Med.

Both Paynter and Fredericks interviewed the specialist. Careful not to tread too heavily in the mine-infested area of medical ethics, even if they did own the specialist, lock, stock and barrel. The medical chaps would always do what you wanted provided you served it up in an acceptable way.

They were used to digging out bullets and stitching up wounds without asking too many questions, and they knew the problems that went with what the department classified as LMF. Lack of Moral Fibre. The mental disturbances of men who had talked or cracked under pressure. And they were just as used to the aberrant behaviour of men who had stuck it out and not talked, but who went to pieces once the pressure was off.

Fredericks avoided any part of the actual discussion, sitting silent and aloof, not even taking off his coat as Paynter pursued his various points. It wasn't the sort of thing he wanted to be involved in. But he considered it his duty to hear what was decided.

The doctor looked at his notes and then at Paynter. 'I listened to the tape of your last conversation with him. I don't think it has any significance either way. You were friendly and considerate and he was – let's say aloof – but he showed no signs of paranoia.'

Paynter nodded. 'That tape was just to establish that prior to anything that might subsequently happen we had treated him reasonably. No antagonism from our side.'

'If you used section 135 of the Mental Health Act the police can remove a mentally ill person from any premises. If you use section 136 any policeman can detain any person found in a public place who he reasonably believes to be mentally disturbed.'

'And after that?'

'He can be held by the police for seventy-two hours and that would give you time to apply to a court for a compulsory admission.' The doctor looked with raised eyebrows at Paynter's face and said softly, 'I assume you'd use your usual devices with the Home Office and that would be that. From what you've told me there's no problem of next-of-kin. Ex-wife is not next-of-kin and the children are too young. You could even consider Crown Court level *in camera* and get indefinite detention without right to review.'

'And how long can we hold him?'

'Provided that it is a recognised mental institution he can be held permanently. And a compulsory patient can be treated against his will.'

'Is our place at Loch Gar a recognised mental institution?'

'Of course.'

And then Fredericks interrupted. 'Are you saying, doctor, that an ordinary policeman with no medical knowledge can seize a citizen in a public place just because he, an unqualified person, considers that citizen mentally disordered?'

'Yes. That's what I'm saying.'

'And he never has to justify the arrest before any court?'

'Exactly. That's what the Mental Health Act 1959 provides for. Some people have suggested that the Act gives an unnecessarily wide power to the police.'

'Is it ever used?'

'Oh. yes. Regularly. Especially in the Greater London area.'

Paynter interrupted. 'If I made arrangements regarding the police, would you attend when the arrest took place?'

'There's no legal need to have a doctor there.'

'I know. You explained that. But just as a back-up.'

The doctor shrugged. 'If that's what the department wished then I'd attend. As you know, when he had his medical at your instigation I taped my talk with him and that establishes my section's concern about signs of paranoia.'

Fredericks sniffed. 'I'd have said he was a psychopath myself.'

The doctor smiled, rather patronisingly. 'On what evidence?'

'The work he did. He was a thug. Killing people ruthlessly.'

'Ah, but he didn't do it out of enjoyment. He killed because people he respected, people in authority, required him to do so. From what you've told me about recent events he is showing acute remorse for the kidnapping of that Arab's children. No psychopath ever shows remorse. He may pretend to if he's caught and he thinks it will help him, but that isn't the case with Rennie. No. Rennie's not a psychopath.'

Paynter said, 'What is he then?'

The doctor said quietly, 'A tough, puritanical man, but otherwise quite normal.'

'No paranoia even?'

'None at all. He feels harassed by authority but that's for a very simple reason. He *is* being harassed by authority. That's why we're here today, gentlemen. We're off the record. I understand your problems and the law provides you with a solution. But let's not be mealy-mouthed about it.'

'Right,' said Fredericks, standing up abruptly. 'I must get on my way. I'll leave you two to discuss the details.'

It was midday on Tuesday when Mary phoned him. She sounded tense.

'Is anything the matter?'

'No, Johnny. Nothing at all. I just wanted to have a word with you.'

'I'll be picking the girls up on Saturday. Will that do?'

'I'd like to see you today.

'OK. I'll come over this evening and see you all.'

'I'd like to see you now. You remember the coffee place you sometimes take the girls to in the High Street?'

'Yes. You mean . . .'

She interrupted quickly. 'I'll be waiting for you there.' And the phone went dead.

She was sitting in the far corner, her back to the restaurant and the windows, and she looked up at him as he pulled out a chair and sat down.

'Can I ask you something, Johnny, something personal?'

'Sure.'

'Do you ever think about the times when you and I were happy?'

'I try not to. But Elizabeth sometimes behaves like you and that reminds me of you when I first met you.'

'I think about you a lot. What a fool I was. Not being responsible. Behaving like a silly schoolgirl. I've tried to hate you, but I've never succeeded. I'm stuck with liking you. And admiring you, even when I don't agree with you. Johnny Rennie – foursquare on to the world.'

'Why are you telling me this?'

'Because I care about you . . .' She shivered involun-tarily. '. . . and to try and pluck up the courage to give you some bad news.'

'What's the bad news?'

The man you told me about, Harry Mason? Is he reli-able?'

'In most ways, yes.'

'Is he a friend of yours?'

'He works with me. I asked him to keep an eye on you if I wasn't around. I mentioned it to you on the phone. Two of the telephone numbers I gave you were his. Home and office.'

'He came to the house this morning. He asked me to warn you about something your people were planning against you.'

'Tell me.'

'A man named Paynter has arranged for you to be taken into custody by a policeman and a doctor. They'll claim that you're insane, and you'll be sent to a place in Scotland. A mental home that's run by your people for their own pur-poses.'

'The one at Loch Gar.'

'Yes. I think that *was* the name he gave.'

'They'd need evidence to do that.'

'They don't. He told me how they intend to do it.'

'Tell me.'

She gave him a garbled but understandable account of what she had been told.

'Did he say when they plan to do this?'

'Paynter told him it would be on a Saturday night so that if there was any struggle it would look like they were arresting a drunk. Mason thought it would be this coming Saturday.'

'Anything else?'

'He said that your phone was almost certainly tapped by now and that I wasn't to discuss it on the phone. He was very upset about it all. He didn't like it. And he was very scared about what would happen to him if they found out that he'd warned you.'

'Must have taken a lot of courage on his part.'

'What are you going to do?'

'It's best I don't tell you, Mary,' Rennie said quietly. 'Then if they ask you, you don't know anything.'

'Mason said you'd leave the country.'

'Can I ask you to do something for me?'

And for the first time in her life she saw tears in his eyes.

'Of course I will. Anything.'

He spoke very slowly. 'If I have to leave the country I'd never be able to come back or they'd have no alternative but to wipe me out. Will you explain some way to the girls that I didn't desert them. That I love them both dearly. And when they're grown up they can come and see me if they want to. Wherever I am.'

And a tear spattered onto the menu he was holding.

'I'll tell them, Johnny. That means you'll go, doesn't it?'

'Probably.'

'They must be terrible people, Johnny. Real animals.'

He half-smiled. 'Until a few weeks back I was one of them, Mary. I'm in no position to criticise.'

'Do you need any money?'

'No. I've got money in various places. More than enough. I've already made arrangements for my pension to be paid directly to you. If they ask you about phoning today, don't deny it. Say we arranged to meet here but I never turned up. And say you had wanted to talk to me about more maintenance and you thought I'd rumbled that and was trying to dodge meeting you.'

She reached out and put her hand on his. 'It seems crazy to be sitting in this crummy little cafe talking about these sorts of things. I can't believe that this is the last time I'll see you.'

'I'll keep in touch but not using my name, and if it's a letter the post-mark won't be relevant and I'll have to beat around the bush with what I say. They'll put a check on all your mail for quite a time.'

'You'd better go, Johnny. You'll have so many things to do.'

He nodded and stood up, and for a moment she hoped he might kiss her. 'You promise to square me off with the girls?'

'Of course I will.'

He nodded and walked away and she saw his eyes checking the other tables and the windows as he went towards the door.

Rennie took a taxi to the nearest Central Line tube station and a train to Redbridge. He waved down a passing taxi which dropped him at the corner of one of the small roads behind Cranbrook Park.

Harry Parks's house was like most of the others. Semi-detached, Victorian and well looked after. As he walked up the stone steps to the front door he saw the lace curtains twitch and guessed that he had been spotted. Harry Parks opened the door before Rennie pressed the bell.

'Come on in, skipper. Lovely to see you.'

Harry took him into the living room and pointed to one of the heavy armchairs.

'What you doin' nowadays, Johnny?'

'The same old thing.' He smiled. 'I need your help.'

'Just say the word, chief. What can I do for you?'

'I want a passport, Harry. Canadian or United States. Doesn't matter which. But it's got to be the real thing and I've got to have it in twenty-four hours.'

'Jesus. You always was the one for the impossible.'

'Can you do it, Harry?'

'Yeah, but it'll cost. Will the department pay?'

'How much?'

'Five hundred quid for the passport and say another hundred for the work. Getting the real thing ain't that easy now I'm retired, and they cost a packet, either of those.'

'How long do you want?'

'Cash?'

'Yes. I'll go down to the bank and draw it out now.'

'Have you got photos?'

'No.'

'Doesn't matter. I can do them upstairs in the studio.'

'So when?'

'You can take it with you today if you'll accept the United States one. I've got one all ready. Let me take a snap or two, and you go and get the cash and get something to read while you're waiting.'

Upstairs in the studio Rennie sat on the straight-backed

chair and Harry Parks measured the distance from the camera lens to his nose. 'Want to get it spot on, skipper. No time for developing and enlarging or reducing. Got to stick to Polaroid.'

Harry took a series of photographs checking each one as it formed, measuring until there were two that could be cut to the correct size.

The local Barclays near Ilford Broadway phoned his Chelsea branch and cleared the transaction before they counted out a thousand pounds in ten-pound notes. He signed for the money and tucked the four bundles of notes into his inside jacket pocket.

For an hour he sat in the park watching some schoolboys playing cricket and then he walked back to Harry Parks's house. Harry Parks had been one of the department's specialists, a talented commercial artist whose skills had been commandeered in wartime and who afterwards had stayed on with SIS. He could produce the right paper, inks, typing, embossing for any kind of document. Ration cards, army orders, security passes, driving licences and all the rest of the forged material that an intelligence organisation needs. And even after his retirement there had been tricky jobs that only Harry could do to a standard that would pass even the most rigorous scientific and complex tests. A chain-smoker, he suffered from chronic bronchitis and lived alone in the house crowded with furniture, framed paintings stacked in piles against every wall and upright surface. His pictures sold readily in local shops and cafes. There had been talk years ago of a wartime love-affair and an illegitimate son but nobody had ever heard any details.

Harry Parks took him upstairs again to the studio and he sat there watching him work on the passport. He worked at a small table with a swivel lamp and a magnifying glass on a stand. On a trolley alongside him were rows of small bottles of inks and colouring ranged in the order of the standard spectrum.

As he worked, Harry said over his shoulder, 'There's an Israeli immigration stamp. D'you want me to take it out? You won't get into an Arab country with this as it is.'

'No. That's OK, Harry. Just leave it. What's my new name?'

'Novaks. Paul Novaks. Born in Pine City, Minnesota. That OK?'

'That's fine. What's the occupation?'

'Says engineer but I can change that if you want.'

'No, that'll do.'

'How's old whatshisname – Peters, Paynter?'

'Paynter. Oh he's still going strong.'

'A sharp bugger he was. If I did a passport for him he always gave it to one of his men first time.' Harry laughed. 'Just to make sure it was OK.'

'He's still much the same. Do they still use you?'

'They did give me odd jobs for a couple of years but I don't hear from them nowadays. As you know they've got a whole bunch of people they use for this kind of work.'

'D'you miss it?'

'No. I make a decent living from the paintings.' He paused. 'How's your old lady?'

'She's fine. We're divorced.'

Harry Parks didn't look up from his work. 'You chaps never stay married long, do you? Either they get fed up hanging around or you've got some little piece in Berlin or Rio de Janeiro. Younger and prettier. Can't blame you. I'd do it myself if I was away all the time.'

It was eleven o'clock before the passport was finished and Rennie counted out seven hundred pounds in ten-pound notes.

'That's very decent of you, Johnny. I'll come down with you and lock up for the night.'

On the doorstep Harry Parks said, 'Take care of yourself, Johnny. Don't let 'em grind you down.'

Rennie smiled. 'You too, Harry.'

It was past one when the taxi dropped him at Sloane Square. The streets were empty as he walked down the deserted King's Road to his rooms. He walked on past the door and then crossed the road, walking back again slowly, checking shop entrances as he went. He realised that if they were already watching him at least it wasn't yet a twenty-four hour surveillance. And that was a good sign.

For the rest of the night he sat at the small table listing the things he had to do. It was a long list and it was already light as he got undressed.

Chapter 26

BY NOON Rennie had drawn all the money from his London bank accounts, and changed it into dollars and dollar traveller's cheques. He had bought one-way airline tickets in the name of Paul Novaks to Paris, Hamburg, Brussels and Toronto. When he had decided where to go the others could be cashed in. The instructions to his overseas banks had been written and posted and he had sold his car for spot cash to a dealer in Battersea.

In the afternoon he bought clothes at Simpson's and Marks and Spencer's and travel-luggage to pack them in. He left the packed cases a couple of hours later at the left-luggage office at Victoria Station.

Back at his rooms he checked again to see if there was anything that was essential to take. His two passports he carried with him permanently, along with his wallet. The tickets were in a plastic folder and the money was in a canvas hold-all. There was nothing to stop him from leaving. Except for two things. He wanted to find out if they really would have come for him and put him away, and secondly, he didn't know where to go.

The only people he knew well anywhere in the world were SIS people. It had always been safer that way. Outsiders wanted to know too much about you. What was your job? What were you doing in wherever you happened to be? SIS men didn't ask questions. They didn't want to know. They provided a place to sleep and a meal. They knew doctors who would sew up a knife wound without asking questions and they could give you a raft of telephone numbers of pretty girls. They could find you a safe place to hide if you were on the run. But not if you were on the run from London. Once you were not one of the 'old firm', even if you'd only retired, you were, at best, just one more outsider.

He moved out from his rooms in darkness at three o'clock the next morning and booked in at a small hotel in Victoria. He spent most of the next few days sleeping and resting and trying not to be aware of the sickening feeling at the pit of his stomach. The feeling that came from the dawning realisation that this wasn't an operation. It was the real thing. He was spending his last few days in the country that he had worked for, holed up in a room in a cheap hotel. Mary and the girls were taken care of but it was unlikely that he would ever see them again. No more trips to the Zoo. No more games of Scrabble. No more stories to be read. No more eager young arms around his neck in reward for some small treat. For the first time in his life John Hamish Rennie was very near the end of his tether. Habit and inbred characteristics were just about keeping his mind on an even keel. But only just. He was very near the end of his mental resources.

He paid three days' rental for a car at a small hire firm in Southwark, and loaded his luggage from the locker at the station. Once they knew he was away they'd check the big hire companies first.

At six o'clock he found a small parking space just off Lower Sloane Street and he walked to the pub that almost faced his rooms. From time to time he glanced out of the steamed-up windows, his fingers wiping a small area clear, but he didn't expect them to come until ten or eleven.

From ten o'clock he watched continuously, a glass of beer in one hand and a ham sandwich in the other. They came at ten twenty-five. Two of them and a driver, in the big Jag from the pool. One was a uniformed policeman and the other was a man he had seen somewhere before. The policeman would be on loan from Special Branch. And as they went inside Rennie remembered the tall one. He was the supervisor at the medical section. And he recalled all that bullshit about paranoia. They must have had some sort of contingency plan all worked out even then. Something on the record to establish that he was unstable. Five minutes later the light went on in his rooms.

A passing constable on foot patrol stopped at the car, opened the door and spoke to the driver, obviously complaining about the car being parked on yellow lines and on a bus route. He saw the constable take out his notebook and then the driver showed him something. Probably his ID card. The notebook was tucked back into the pocket and the constable nodded and moved on.

Rennie walked out of the side entrance of the pub and back to his rented car. Two hours later he cashed in his airline tickets at Gatwick and booked a seat on the early-morning plane to Amsterdam. He used his United States passport and booked in for the night at the airport Hilton in the name of Paul Novaks. He tried to sleep but spent most of the night pacing the room. Several times he picked up the phone to change his flight to some other place than Amsterdam. He knew Berlin better and Rome too. And there was the sunshine of the Spanish coast from Malaga to Alicante. But in those few weeks he had felt strangely at home in Amsterdam. Despite what he had been involved in, there was a sanity about the people and a calmness about those medieval buildings that gave him comfort. And there was the room and the girl. He could try it for a few weeks. She would be someone to talk to.

Just once he started dialling the number of his old house before he slammed down the receiver. The temptation to talk to the girls just one last time was constantly there. But it was self-indulgence and by now the phone would be tapped. Rennie found it almost impossible to accept the role of being the hunted not the hunter. Always before there had been the righteous cause to give a patina of innocence to deception and subterfuge, but without that it all seemed degrading and inhuman. His mind was no longer decisive and his reactions changed constantly from blazing anger to despair, from guilt to humiliation. He didn't belong in this strange new scenario.

At Schiphol he took a taxi to Warmoesstraat and slowly unloaded his bags. It took two journeys to get them to the top of the stairs. He walked down slowly and paid off the driver. When he turned to look up the stairs it seemed as if they were moving.

The ascent up the narrow wooden stairs seemed interminable and he could feel the sweat pouring down his face as he stood outside the door. It seemed to take a long time for his hand to find the brass handle. As his fingers closed round it the door opened and he was vaguely aware of the girl standing there. He leaned against the door-jamb, his hand feeling for some support, and not finding any his body slid down to the floor as his knees slowly gave way.

As he tried to work out where he was, he saw her standing looking out of the window and as the bed creaked she turned quickly to look at him. He was vaguely aware of her hand stroking his face before he passed out again. He tried to speak but no words came out.

When he woke again the light was on in the room and she was sitting on the bed beside him, holding his hand.

'How're you feeling, Johnny? Just nod if you're feeling better.'

His mouth and lips were dry and his voice was a croak as he tried to smile as he said, 'I'm fine.'

'You idiot,' she said, 'you're not fine. And I've been so worried.' He could see tears in her eyes.

'What's going on?' he said.

'You passed out two days ago. I got a doctor. He said you were suffering from exhaustion. What the hell have you been doing to get into this state?'

He shrugged. 'Just wear and tear.'

She shook her head in disbelief. 'You're going to drink a bowl of soup. Not tinned. The real stuff.'

The doctor called in twice during the next week. Probing in slow precise English as to what might have caused his patient's collapse, and getting nowhere.

After the second visit she had walked down to the street with the doctor.

'How is he, doctor?'

'He's a very strong man so physically there's nothing to

210

worry about. But mentally I'm not so sure.'

'In what way?'

'To be perfectly frank – I don't know. But there's something wrong there. Something stored up. There's a big, big scream inside that man. Some day it's going to come out. And I don't know what will happen then.'

'What could help him?'

The doctor shrugged. 'Getting him to talk. He won't talk to me. He's obviously experienced at hiding his feelings. He's better at evading questions than I am at asking them.' He turned and looked at the girl. 'Maybe you could do it.'

'But I don't know what to ask.'

'I don't think you need to know anything. You just need to get him to talk. It's a bit like cutting open a boil to let out the pus.' He paused as he looked at her face. 'You're fond of him, aren't you?'

'Yes. I care about him a lot.'

'I think that that's why you might succeed where I've failed.' He looked down the street and then back to the girl's face. 'I'm only guessing, but I think I'm right – I don't think anyone has cared for that man for a long, long time. Something, or somebody, has drained his batteries over the years. Maybe you could charge them for him.'

'I'll try.'

The doctor smiled. 'I'm sure you will contact me if you feel he needs anything.'

'I will.'

'Good luck.'

'Thank you.'

By the end of the week Rennie was fit enough to go for short walks in the autumn sunshine, sitting in small nearby cafes, drinking coffee and eating cream cakes.

The girl was trying desperately not to hurry any attempt to persuade him to talk, or to choose a wrong moment. Although they chatted as they ate and drank she was aware that his responses were strained and only made with great effort. She was also aware of his unease when they were away from the room, his eyes roving over the people they passed as if he were looking for someone. Although he was physically much fitter he seemed to be retreating mentally a little more each day. When they were back in the room he lay on the bed, his eyes closed, but he wasn't asleep, and when he opened his eyes he just lay there inert, staring unseeing at the ceiling.

As his condition deteriorated she asked the doctor to call again. He stayed for almost half an hour and afterwards he talked to her on the stairs.

'I've left some pills for him. He says he won't take them. They're Valium and they could probably calm him down. See if you can persuade him to take them. It's important that he should.'

'What's the matter with him, do you think?'

'It's obviously depression. Not just feeling down but clinical depression. I want to break it up. It could give him a chance to relax and stop all those wheels grinding away so relentlessly in his mind.' He paused. 'If you could get him to talk . . . to unburden himself a little, it could help a lot.'

'I've been afraid of making things worse.'

'You won't do that. He's too deep inside himself already. He should really be in hospital. I suggested it but he wouldn't cooperate.' He paused. 'I'm very worried about him.'

'Tell me.'

For several moments the doctor was silent and then he said quietly, 'I'd say that he was potentially suicidal.'

'Oh God.'

'Are you sure that you can cope with him on your own? I could consider having him removed to a clinic whether he agrees or not.'

'Oh don't do that. I can cope. I'm sure I can.'

'OK. But if you change your mind let me know.'

'I won't change my mind.'

The doctor nodded and made his way down the narrow stairs.

She had persuaded him to take the pills for two days and when they had finished their evening meal and they were drinking their coffee she said softly, 'Will you tell me what went wrong, Johnny?'

She half expected a dismissive shake of the head but he put down his cup and looked at her across the table.

212

'I guess I owe you an explanation, sweetie, after all the trouble I've caused.'

You don't *owe* me anything and you've been no trouble. I'd just like to help, that's all.'

'It would take a long time to explain. And it's all a bit mixed up.'

'I've got all the time in the world for you, John Rennie, so tell me what it's all about.'

It was past midnight when he finished telling her. Not only the recent events in Amsterdam but of the years before. She asked very few questions but she reached out and covered his hand with hers when he sometimes came to a halt or found something difficult to explain. When he stopped she said softly, 'We're a bit alike, you and I, aren't we?'

'In what way?'

'Inside we're both terrible puritans. Not liking the world we see around us. But in practice we both indulge in the very things we quite genuinely despise. You in your dirty-tricks, and me in my dope and squatting and general bumming around.'

'I guess so. But yours does no harm to other people. Mine's on a different scale.'

She smiled. 'You were very cross with me once when I said that me smoking hash did nobody any harm but me.'

'I'm sorry.'

'Don't be sorry, Johnny. What I've done isn't worth talking about. What about you? What are you going to do?'

'Do you mind if I hang on here for a bit while I sort myself out?'

'You don't have to ask me, Johnny, *I'm* the visitor, not you. This is your place.'

'Tell me something, Joanna. You said to me once that you didn't like the society we live in because it doesn't care about its losers. What did you mean by that? Do you mean that if a man doesn't make an effort to support himself that the state should do it for him?'

'No. I mean that there are tens of thousands of people in the USA and Europe who try very hard to succeed but for one reason or another – genes or environment or maybe ill-health – they don't make it. I don't think it's right that those people and their families should be without food or shelter or medical care. And it's not the state that should help them. The state is a myth. It's the rest of us who should help them. And willingly, not grudgingly. And we should care about people in other countries who die because they lack basic medicine and food. Babies die who could live for a month on what we throw away in a couple of days.'

'Are you describing Communism?

'Yes,' she said, defiantly. 'The snag is, that if you believe Communism would work everybody assumes you are pro-Moscow. The Russians aren't Communists at all. They're just tyrants, dictators. With love it would work.' She paused and said lamely, 'I'm sure it would, Johnny.' She hesitated for a moment and then she said, 'What made you so sure that the establishment was always right? Especially when you had a grandstand view of the things they got up to.'

'I think it was reaction against the people who wanted to bring the country down by revolution and force.'

'What attracted you to that kind of work in the first place?'

'It's a gradual process. You don't just decide that that's what you want to do. They look out all the time for people who could be useful in one way or another. You're asked to do something, and if you do it well you're given something else to do. You kind of drift into it. It seems like that anyway but in fact it's very carefully controlled. Testing you out without you knowing it.'

'But you must have liked it or you wouldn't have stayed. And you wouldn't have been successful.'

'It's not a question of liking it. You see what's going on behind the scenes and you want to play your part in stopping it.'

'But isn't it all rather phoney or exaggerated? Is all that much really happening?'

Rennie shrugged. 'Right now some man at one of the KGB schools will be under training for a mission to find out some industrial secret in a plant in Cardiff or London or somewhere in Britain. Another man will be looking over a list of people who run so-called peace movements. Deciding how to penetrate them and turn the protest into

214

violence and subversion. Thousands of highly-trained people spend all their working hours planning how to destroy the whole fabric of society in Britain. And others will be doing the same for every country in the non-Soviet world. There's no question of exaggeration. It's fact. It suits some people to pretend it isn't happening. But it is. And I wish it wasn't. That's why I wanted to do my bit to stop it.'

'But isn't it up to ordinary people to decide what they want? They won't be conned by a few Russians.'

Rennie smiled. 'The Russians don't do the conning themselves, they just control and direct the people who do it.'

'What people?'

'All sorts of people. People who openly rant and rave in public about everything the government does. And the really dangerous ones. The quiet ones who weasel their way into any group of people who have a genuine grievance.

'Groups against the bomb, civil liberty groups, strikers with a genuine grievance. As soon as they start, the undercover people move in and encourage violence. The general public end up losing sympathy with the causes but the media people, newspapers and TV, give the spoilers space and air-time to put over their picture of class-hatred and defiance of the law. The media call it balance. But it isn't. It just sells newspapers. If you had anything good to say about the country or the government, they wouldn't be interested. They want scandal and violence.'

'But if they don't convince the public, what does it matter?'

'It matters because they are trying to destroy the public faith in democracy. If some clerk in a government office leaks a secret document to the press, he says he did it in the public interest and the newspaper claims that too. The fact that the clerk signed the Official Secrets Act swearing to maintain confidentiality is seen as a restriction on civil liberties. It's not just that they do it, but they pretend that their breach of the Act is from the highest motives.

'And behind all these dupes are the real manipulators. The quiet ones who never speak in public but whose role is to keep the political pot boiling. And behind them the KGB and all the others who murder and blackmail in order to destroy us.'

'What made you change your mind about all this?'

'I don't think I did change my mind about it. I still think somebody has to fight them. All of them. But not me any more.'

'Why?' she said quietly.

For several moments he didn't speak. Then he sighed and said, 'It started with you when you said how honest I was. The woman at the gallery, Adele Palmer, said the same. For some reason it set me thinking. I realised that in my private life I was honest. Genuinely honest. But in my work there was no room for honesty. I justified that by accepting that somebody had to do what I did. To protect society. The public.' He sighed. 'And for some reason my rationalising started falling apart . . . I don't know why.'

'I do.'

'Tell me then.'

'It was the little girl. The Arab's daughter. For you that was going too far.'

'If I want to stay honest in your eyes then I have to say no . . . it wasn't just that. In fact until I was telling you tonight about all that had happened, I wasn't really sure what the turning point was.'

'What was it, Johnny? Tell me.'

'I didn't like the kidnapping of Said's children. There were other ways of dealing with the problem. And in the end the kidnapping didn't help in getting Mason back. No . . . what really brought it home was the incident with the coffins. Not just the sadism, the cruelty, but the fact that they did it to *my* family. That may sound just selfish but it isn't. It was a signpost for me that they had too much power. They didn't have to justify what they did to anybody. They just had to give an order to somebody and it was done. Whoever did it wouldn't have questioned what they were asked to do. It was just a job. And they did it. Just like I had done it so many many times. The Nazis on trial at Nuremberg gave that as their excuse. They were just obeying orders.' He paused and said softly, 'Those people who were my masters were more sophisticated than I was.

216

And I guess that I've just grown up. What was tolerable for me as a young man isn't tolerable now I'm older.' He paused. 'Or maybe I'm still busy rationalising my own behaviour. Who knows.'

'Does it help to have talked about it?'

'I'm not sure. I think so. It's a relief to have said it aloud instead of it churning around inside my head.'

'You are honest, Johnny. Don't doubt that. It's a nasty world we live in especially the bit you've been living in.'

'And what are we all going to do about it, honey?'

She shook her head. 'I don't know, Johnny. You can't just go around telling people to be nice to one another.'

'That's what Jesus Christ did.'

'Sure. And look what they did to *him*.'

'So it's all hopeless?'

'No way. It's not hopeless.'

'Tell me what we have to do.'

'We have to live our lives so that we are never tempted to do anyone any harm. We give up all forms of aggression as individuals. Greed, ambition, indifference are all a kind of personal aggression. We just have to live quietly and lovingly.'

'On that small farm you wanted. Just enough to get by.'

She smiled. 'Funny you remembering that. But you're right. That's one way.' She shrugged. 'It would suit me.'

'Truly, or is it just a dream thing?'

'It's a dream thing all right. But it's real for me.'

'So why not do it?'

She sighed. 'I couldn't do it alone. I'd be scared.'

'So do it with me.'

She lifted her head and looked at his face as she said softly, 'Don't tease me, Johnny.'

'I'm not teasing. I mean it. Seriously.'

'You mean you could turn your back on all your old life? The excitement. The power. The people you know.'

'I've done that already, my dear. I've nothing to lose. I've lost already.'

'But on your own you could see the world.'

'I've seen the world – I didn't like the look of it.'

She looked at his face for a long time and then said quietly, 'I'd love it, Johnny. I wouldn't be a nuisance.'

217

'So why are there tears in your eyes?'

'Because I love you, Johnny Rennie. I've loved you for forty-nine days. And it all seems too good to be true.'

'Where shall we have our farm?'

'We'd have to raise a loan first.'

'I've got all the money we'll need. So where do we go?'

'You say. I'll go wherever you say.'

Rennie put his hand in his jacket pocket and took out the two passports. One British, one United States. He pointed at the green one. 'That's the only one I can use. So let's go to your place.'

'Where in the States?'

'Have you ever been to Vermont?'

'No.'

'Let's go there then.'

'Do you like it there?'

'I've never been there.'

She laughed. 'So why choose Vermont?'

'A long time ago I heard a song – I think it was Glenn Miller – it was called "Moonlight in Vermont". I've always remembered it, and I've always wanted to go there. It sounded special.'

She smiled. 'My dream – the little farm. Your dream – Vermont. It sounds a great combination.'

'Let's start planning.'

She looked at him quizzically, her head to one side just like young Mary sometimes did. 'Do you like me at all, Johnny?'

'Yes. More than like.'

'But not love?'

'You once said you liked it when I came here. That it made you feel safe. I feel that about you. I like being with you. And I feel safe with you.'

'Safe from what?'

'Safe from hurt. Safe from the rest of the world.'

She smiled. 'That's not a bad start, is it?'

'For me it's pretty good. I hope it is for you.'

'It is, Johnny Rennie. It is.'

It was already turning from autumn to winter and there was

a cold wind as he walked over the bridge, and then he saw her, running towards him, her long blonde hair streaming out behind her like a palomino's mane.'

She was panting as she got up to him, smiling as she waved a large brown envelope.

'He's found what we wanted, Johnny. It's perfect.'

'Who's found what?'

'It's a long letter from daddy. He's found us a place. In Vermont. On Lake Champlain. There's photographs and maps and everything. Even the name is romantic.'

'What's the name?'

'South Hero. Isn't that great?'

He smiled. 'Let's go and have a board meeting.'

They had done the calculations, pored over the maps and field plans and had tried hard not to be over-influenced by the beautiful scenery in the photographs. But Johan de Vries had done a good job. It was exactly what they wanted. She could barely keep still, she was so pleased and excited.

'Shall I phone him tonight, Johnny? We could go to one of the hotels and use an international kiosk.'

'Yes. Let's do that. He'll be delighted to know you'll be back so soon.'

'There's just one thing,' and her face looked serious.

'What's that?'

'I want us to do something before we decide. I want us to look down the other end of the telescope.'

'How do we do that?'

'I want us to be honest with one another. I want both of us to look at it from the other's point of view. And say out loud what we think are the snags. Not for ourselves but for the other one.'

He looked at her fondly and reached out for her hand. 'Tell me why we should do that?'

'Because I think there are a lot of disadvantages for you in all this. And none for me. You ought to think about them before we plunge.'

For long moments he looked at her face and then he said softly, 'I love you, Joanna de Vries.'

'Do you mean that, Johnny?'

'I do.'

'What would be your description of loving someone?'

He shrugged. 'A very simple one. That you would rather anything bad happened to you than to the other person.'

'So,' she smiled. 'Let's be Devil's Advocates for each other. You start.'

He sighed. 'There are three disadvantages for you that I'm aware of. The first is that I would like to ask you to marry me. But I can't. With my phoney passport and no supporting documents we'd be caught at first base. That's unfair on you and not too good for your parents.'

She nodded. 'Go on.'

'Secondly, you might get tired of me. I'm much older than you for one thing and . . .'

'Forget that,' she said. 'It's rubbish.'

'And thirdly you might find the life boring or too much hard work,' he paused. 'And one more thing I've just remembered. We could never be sure that I wasn't going to be exposed.'

'The only bit that matters to me is the marrying bit. But that could come right in time. There's ways of putting these things right. Daddy might be able to help. But I'd like us to pretend to be married so far as the outside world is concerned. Just a wedding ring and me with your name.'

'I'm sorry that it has to be so messy but that's fine with me. What about the other snags?'

She shook her head. 'They don't matter. None of them.'

'Your turn in the box then.'

'I've only got two points. One is big and the other one's sort of medium. Let me do the mediun one first. You've been terribly down because of what's happened to you. Do you think when you've recovered properly and you're fit that you won't miss your old work?'

'I won't miss it for a moment. They wouldn't have me back anyway. They'd sooner cut my throat.'

'Maybe. But other intelligence services would be glad to have you. I bet the CIA would have you like a shot.'

He shook his head vehemently. 'Forget it. What's the other thing?'

It was several seconds before she spoke. 'Is there any

220

chance you still love your ex-wife?'

'No. She's a good mother and a nice lady but she's not for me.'

'And the girls? I know you love them.'

'Yes,' he said quietly, 'I love the girls and I'll be sad sometimes when I think about them. I shall miss them terribly. I do already. But I think you're forgetting something fundamental.'

'What's that?'

'Once they decided to certify me as insane there was no choice left for me. I had no choice but to leave or go into a mental institution. It's better this way. If things work out I might see the girls again some day.'

'You don't think SIS or whatever they're called would forgive you?'.

He smiled. 'It's a nice gentle word "forgive". No, they're not designed for forgiving. And I don't want their forgiveness.'

'I want you to be so happy, Johnny.'

He leaned across the table and for the first time ever he kissed her on the lips.

Johan de Vries met them at Kennedy and drove them the next day to the small farmstead at South Hero. When they went to the realtor to complete the deal he smiled as he gave Rennie the big buff envelope. The farmstead had already been bought by Johan de Vries and the deeds were in the names of Paul Novaks and his wife Joanna Veronica Novaks. The realtor, enjoying his role of Fairy Prince, found it entirely fitting that Joanna Veronica Novaks should burst into tears.

Chapter 27

THE TYPESCRIPT and its packing lay untidily on Fredericks's desk. He was no longer responsible for FO/SIS liaison. He had been transferred to the Foreign Office with a two-grade promotion. He stood with his hands in his trouser pockets, rocking slowly on his heels.

'Why haven't you consulted Mayhew on this? It's nothing to do with me.'

'I thought you might have a view.'

'I do, dear boy, I do. But it's not my domain any longer. It's yours – and Mayhew's.'

'I'd be obliged if you gave me your views. Unofficially of course.'

Fredericks smiled but not with his eyes. 'Are you scared of what Mayhew might start? A cosy little Commission of Enquiry to keep his new friends in the FO happy. A show of his independence from SIS. Is that it?'

'Yes.'

'Well at least you're frank about it. Some wouldn't be.' *He waved towards the untidy package on his desk.* 'How damaging would it be?'

'Very damaging.'

'More than Mason's?'

'Oh far worse. Mason wasn't dirty-tricks.'

Fredericks pursed his lips in disapproval of the phrase. 'Is it accurate?'

'There are some errors on dates but nothing more than that.'

Fredericks sighed and looked at his neat black shoes. 'Probably compiled from memory.' *He looked up quickly at Paynter.* 'D'you think he'd use it?'

'I'm sure he would.'

'Did your chap trace where he is?'

'No. He's still looking. I called a halt as soon as I got this stuff. It's a small area and I've no doubt we could trace him in the next few weeks. But he's probably using some other name.'

'Well he's got you by the short and curlies, my friend. No doubt about that. He was on our – your side of the fence when Mason was scribbling away for those wretched Arabs. He saw the panic that caused.'

'So what do we do?'

Fredericks laughed sharply. 'We don't do anything. But if I were you, I'd take every paper on that operation and shove it in the shredder. Then cremate it. And if there's any chance of sending up a smoke-signal to your old friend Rennie – then do it. And don't go near him ever again.' Fredericks raised his eyebrows in dismissal and Paynter got up, gathered up the package and headed across the thick carpet to the door.

At the door he turned and said, 'Thanks for your help, Freddie.' Fredericks ignored him, looking out of the window, watching the Scots Guards march past. The band was playing 'Auld Lang Syne'.